MARKED MAN . . .

"We have the situation well in hand now," Barnes said.

The other man shifted in the booth. "Well in hand? You've got some madman from Costa Bella sitting in the California warehouse. You've got a pilot who's ready to flip out. And you've got a highly trained assassin somewhere wondering what the hell is going on."

"Let's take it step by step," Barnes said, falling back on his years of Agency training. "Rojas is not a problem. We'll have him out of the country shortly. Dr. Lee will be attended to very soon. I agree that he has become a dangerous liability. We both knew that sooner or later he would have to go. Now's the time. And as for Gavin—he's as good as dead."

Barnes opened up the leather portfolio and extracted a large photo. It was a blowup of Gavin's last official photograph, taken when he started with the Agency eight years before.

The other man's thick fingers held the print carefully by the edges. "You want me to put out a general contract on this guy, right?"

Barnes nodded. "Gavin should never walk out of Costa Bella. But if he does, get him."

T the #1 ERMINATOR
MERCENARY KILL
by John Quinn

PINNACLE BOOKS **NEW YORK**

THE TERMINATOR #1: MERCENARY KILL

Copyright © 1982 by Dennis Rodriguez

All rights reserved, including the right to reproduce this book or portions thereof in any form.

An original Pinnacle Books edition, published for the first time anywhere.

First printing, September 1982

ISBN: 0-523-41695-4

Cover illustration by Gil Cohen

Printed in the United States of America

PINNACLE BOOKS, INC.
1430 Broadway
New York, New York 10018

MERCENARY KILL

prologue _____

Gavin was the gas man.

No one noticed him. He wore light gray twill shirt and pants, a blue Dodgers baseball cap, and a tool belt. Stitched in flowing script above his left-hand shirt pocket was the name Bob.

Traffic was light on Biscayne Boulevard and he crossed at the corner of Thirty-fourth Street. He held a clipboard to which were affixed a few printed forms.

The humid Miami heat was staggering.

Gavin entered the main lobby of the Vizcaya Apartments and headed directly for the meter-and-valve installation. The shut-off for apartment 3-C was clearly labeled.

Gavin turned off the gas for 3-C.

He left the building, recrossed Biscayne Boulevard, and entered an apartment building directly across from the Vizcaya. He took the stairs to the third floor. He let himself into the first apartment to the left of the staircase, closed the door, and tossed the baseball cap onto the sofa.

He fished a beer from the cooler by the window that overlooked Biscayne Boulevard.

He reached out and flicked on the audio surveillance gear that brought in apartment 3-C, across the street, loud and clear. He waited, listening to their idle talk. A ball game was on TV.

An hour later Alexei asked the others if they wanted coffee. One no, one yes. Alexei went into the kitchen and Gavin could hear him swearing loudly in Russian, his voice scratchy in Gavin's receiver. The range didn't work. Gavin knew why.

It took them fifteen minutes to decide to call the gas company and complain, in heavily accented English. The gas company promised a repairman before the day was out.

Gavin could do better than that. He had another beer and waited an hour. Then he pulled out his work shirt and tucked the .45 into his waistband. He picked up his clipboard and left the apartment. He crossed Biscayne and entered the Vizcaya Apartments.

Upstairs in 3-C was Ivanovich with his two bodyguards, Alexei and Pasha. Ivanovich was in charge of infiltrating Cuban agents into the United States, and was a colonel in the KGB. Alexei and Pasha were also KGB, built like beer kegs, merciless as morgue slabs.

It was time for everyone to earn their pay. Gavin knocked on the door.

Alexei opened before Pasha was ready. He must've wanted that cup of coffee pretty bad, Gavin thought. Pasha should have been stationed in the other room, his weapon ready. It was standard procedure. But when Alexei swung open the door after checking Gavin through the peep, Pasha was right behind him, walking out of the kitchen.

Gavin's first round rolled back Alexei's skull and blew pink spray. His second round caught Pasha before he had time to react. The .45 slug tore through Pasha's neck, mushrooming Pasha's head off his shoulders.

Gavin heard a noise in the other room as Ivanovich made a dash for the bedroom. Gavin's last round took him through the side and banged him against the wall hard. When Ivanovich slid down Gavin tossed the .45 to the floor and left the apartment. An old lady was standing in the hall looking around. Her hand clutched her dressing gown to her throat. "Did you hear anything?" she asked Gavin.

"Sounded like gun shots," he said, "Or a car backfiring."

one _____

They had been marching for two days.

Jorge de Leon shifted his pack and thought about the beers he would consume as soon as this was over. Chilled beers, of course. That was a habit he had picked up in the United States, where beverages were always served cold.

In Costa Bella, most of the men still preferred their drinks, even beer, *a tiempo,* "at room temperature." De Leon let his mind play with images of tall frosty glasses filled with foamy beer leading the way.

"Alto!" De Leon glanced up. Colonel Rojas had signaled for the column to prepare an ambush. De Leon squinted against the glare and was able to make out a trail of dust approaching them. Surely not the rebels—their tactics did not involve such sophisticated methods as motorized transportation. De Leon gripped his M-14 and trotted to Colonel Rojas.

"What are we doing?"

Rojas smiled. "We are preparing an

ambush, *teniente*. The rebels are coming. It is our job."

De Leon wanted to tell him that there were no rebels, only peasants fighting to survive. But Rojas already knew that. The only people interested in that information were the *norteamericanos*, who were considering supplying Rojas and the other monsters loose in Costa Bella with even more arms.

De Leon stared in Rojas's bloodshot eyes and saw the yellow flicker of hatred there. De Leon had no choice. He had to go along with whatever Rojas said or face instant death for insubordination.

As de Leon hurried to his position he thought, this will be the last time. As soon as they returned to Bahia his report could be sent. His report would be clear and to the point. The Costa Bellan Government is a bloodthirsty tyranny, and the resistance of the citizenry is nothing more than self-defense.

As he took his position he could make out the small vehicle approaching. It was a jeep, open, with four passengers. Perhaps even Rojas could see that they were civilians, harmless, unaware of what they were getting into.

But Rojas gave the order to fire and the staccato bursts of fire shattered the jeep's windshield and sent the vehicle bouncing off the road. The driver was a man, but the other three passengers were women.

The men approached the jeep slowly, as if there were some danger. De Leon shouldered his rifle and stared at the bloodied bodies. Flies were already settling on the torn flesh, gathering around the puckered wounds.

"Finish them," Rojas said to de Leon.

"What?"

"Finish them. Use your .45. A round in each head, if you please. I hate to see such suffering."

The four bodies appeared to be Americans, or Europeans. De Leon realized that something was very wrong. "But colonel," he began.

Rojas put his hand on his own .45. "Will you not obey a simple order?" He asked. De Leon realized that nothing would give Rojas greater pleasure than shooting him on the spot.

There was no choice. De Leon consoled himself with the observation that all four appeared to be dead already. He pulled out his .45. It had never seemed to weigh as much before. Now it felt as if it required every bit of his strength to lift it.

The older woman in the back seat moaned.

Rojas grinned. "You see? You are an angel of mercy, my friend. You must end their pain. It is the Christian thing to do."

De Leon put a round into each victim, in

the back of their heads. He felt his stomach turning as each skull seemed to dissolve as the round tore through the skin and bone with an awful sound.

De Leon turned and fell to his knees and emptied himself. His retching continued long after there was anything in his stomach. He could hear Rojas behind him, searching the bodies.

"Ah, we have made an error," he said. "Look at this."

De Leon turned, sitting now, his arms locked around his legs. "Nuns," Rojas said. "Nuns and one priest."

Rojas was holding their identification cards, his smile lewd with bloodlust. De Leon scrambled to his feet and stood there, shaking with a sudden bone-chilling cold.

"We must hope and pray," Rojas said, "that they were in a state of grace."

two _____

Presidential Assistant Jed Anderson was thirty-two thousand feet above the cornfields of Kansas, stoned out of his mind. As he stared at his ashen reflection under the sickening light of the forward head aboard *Air Force One,* he vowed never again to get so loaded when the President was in such a bad mood.

There was no question about that, Anderson thought. The Old Man was ready to kick ass and Anderson's was very handy. That was one reason that he had spent as much of the flight as possible cooped up in the head. Smoking that joint with Blair after the press conference had been a mistake.

The famous smile and happy-farm-boy manner that the President used on the press and the public often vanished as soon as he was alone with his men. Especially when he was pissed off, Anderson thought glumly.

Anderson sighed, ran the cold water tap,

scooped up the chill water in his palms, and splashed his face. Then he straightened, smoothed his lank brown hair, and adjusted his eyeglasses. He looked older than his age and that was all right with Jed Anderson. Nobody liked a young guy with all the answers, or even a young guy who thought he had all the answers. Jed Anderson was happiest when he was mistaken for a piece of furniture. He didn't want to rock the boat.

Paulson was the first person Anderson saw when he came out of the head. "Get it together," Paulson snapped. "The Old Man's been looking for you and he's not happy."

"I was in the head."

Paulson sneered. "That's terrific. Go tell the President."

Jed Anderson smiled back at Paulson but what he wanted most to do was utter three simple words to the man. Someday he would, and the look on Paulson's face would have made the wait worthwhile. "Paulson," Anderson would say, "you're fired."

The President spun around in his conference chair when Jed Anderson entered the forward cabin used mainly for meetings. "Anderson," the President said, "You know what sort of day I've had?"

"Well—no, Mr. President."

"You might find this worthwhile—in case you ever think about running for office," the President added. His hands were tented, his elbows resting on the table. His gaze was just to the left of Jed Anderson's face. Jed was used to it.

The President spoke as if he were alone, and Jed Anderson relaxed. The President often did this. He needed to air his thoughts. He needed to talk to someone who wouldn't carry the conversation anywhere.

"What do you know about Costa Bella?" the President asked suddenly.

Jed Anderson swallowed. He reined in what was left of his mind and channeled its energies into the Facts Department. "Costa Bella," Jed Anderson said. "Bounded on the south by El Salvador, on the north and west by Guatemala. A poor, underdeveloped, Central American country. Mountain ranges running north and south, I believe—" Jed Anderson noticed that the President wasn't listening.

"Jed," the President finally said, "Earlier today I saw the secretary of state. He wants us to take a firm stand in the fighting down there. Seems he's got information that the civil uprising is Communist led. Backed by Cuba and Nicaragua."

Jed Anderson nodded. He had heard the same reports.

The President shifted in his chair. "And the secretary of defense is pushing me to grant military aid. Can't blame him. He's got all those industrialists on his back, whining for defense contracts."

"Are you going to do it, Mr. President?"

The President looked up sharply. Jed Anderson's question had snapped him out of his rambling.

"Jed, I want you to arrange a meeting tomorrow morning with Jack Duffy."

"Duffy?" Jed Anderson knew most of the President's men, and the name Duffy was a new one.

"Works at the Justice Department. He's doing a special job for me."

"Yes, Mr. President." Jed Anderson's mouth was dry and his forehead was beaded with sweat.

"That's all, Jed," the President said.

Jed nodded and turned to leave. As he opened the door leading to the communications area the President said, "And one more thing, Jed."

Jed Anderson turned around. "Yes, Mr. President?"

"I wouldn't get too friendly with the press if I were you. Especially that wire-service fellow, Blair. I understand that you two knew each other at Rutgers. I'd soft-pedal that relationship for a while."

Jed Anderson swallowed so loudly that it sounded like a rifle shot. "Yes, Mr. President." And then he left.

*   *   *

The next afternoon at two-thirty Jack Duffy sat in a bar in Georgetown, watched the would-be Beautiful People play with each other, and thought about his earlier meeting with the President.

He ordered another Chivas—double, neat— and sipped it slowly. The President hadn't been angry. Nor had he shown any signs of displeasure. He had come to the point immediately. "We've run out of time, Duffy. I need the report now."

There was a problem. Duffy's field man, Jorge de Leon, had been out of touch for a few days. He had explained this to the President.

"Duffy, there's nothing to discuss. I have to act with or without your report. I have perhaps a week. Then I'm going to have to act."

The pressure on the President to make the "Costa Bella Decision," as it was termed that morning in the *Washington Post*, was obvious. The President had taken a hard line against Communist expansion in the hemisphere. The evidence in Costa Bella, as far as everyone knew, pointed to the fine hands of Fidel Castro and the *Sandinistas* of Nicaragua. Was the President going to stand by and let another communist takeover happen?

Duffy loosened his tie and unbuttoned his collar. He was putting on weight. His shirt collar was uncomfortably snug. He sipped more Scotch and watched a beautiful, leggy blonde sweep by his booth, nose in the air, conscious of the hot male eyes following her every move.

The expanding warmth of the whiskey relaxed Duffy. He turned his head slowly from side to side, easing the tension that had built up during his meeting with the President.

He sincerely wished that he had never heard of Costa Bella, or Jorge de Leon, or any of it. Duffy was comfortable in his niche in the Justice Department. Life was good; and all he had to do was perform in a competent fashion and it would continue to be good.

Duffy smiled. The waitress thought he was smiling at her. She came over to the table to see if he wanted another drink. Duffy had no idea what was bothering her. He hadn't even been conscious of the smile on his face.

It was a curious habit. Duffy smiled when the tension got great, when the stress of a situation made other men bellow with rage or weep softly into their beers.

Duffy was feeling the stress and the tension and he knew it. He'd felt it most during the President's special briefing—a technicolor horror show, more than Duffy thought he'd be able to take.

The President had said, "I want you to see this film, Duffy. It will show you the

importance of this mission." The President
had sent Duffy two floors below the ground
level of the White House to the projection
room used for intelligence films. There, in
upholstered theater chairs, he had watched
the film along with Jed Anderson, the Presidential assistant.

"These films were shot by members of
the Costa Bellan military," Anderson had
told him. "I hope you have a strong stomach."

The film began with a close-up of a Costa
Bellan Government soldier wearing U.S.
surplus combat gear. He was lying on his
face and it looked as if someone had caved
in the back of his head with a sledge hammer. The flics were thick and moving.
Duffy was glad the film was not shot with
sound.

"The government forces are taking loss-
es," Anderson had said. "Substantial loss-
es, if we can believe them." The film now
showed a stack of government soldiers,
lying atop each other, neatly, as if awaiting shipment somewhere. Judging from
the newness of the soles of their combat
boots, Duffy figured that they were raw
recruits, probably ambushed their first or
second time out.

The next few scenes were of the rebels,
men dressed in everything from designer
jeans to the white billowing pants worn
by the Costa Bellan peasants. It appeared
that many more rebels were being killed

than government troops. Rebel bodies,
however, were not stacked neatly. More
often than not the cameraman caught them
just before they were scooped into mass
graves by bulldozers. Some shots were of
the bodies already in the trenches.

When it was over, Anderson had grinned
and said, "War's hell."

But that had little to do with Duffy's
present problem.

The problem was that Duffy couldn't contact Jorge de Leon. De Leon was Duffy's
man in Costa Bella, an army officer who
had been educated in the United States. De
Leon had agreed to supply a report to Duffy
on the political-military situation in Costa
Bella, but de Leon hadn't been heard from
in weeks.

The President had said, "We're going to
have to bring CIA into it."

Duffy had protested. "But what's the
point?" he had asked. "The reason for a de
Leon in the first place is to have an independent report on the situation. You've
already got the CIA report," he had said to
the President. "Bringing CIA in now would
eliminate any chance of getting an independent opinion from de Leon."

The President had been unmoved. "Got
no choice," he had told Duffy. "For all we
know, de Leon's been killed in action. I've
told Barnes at CIA to handle it. He'll locate

your man, get the report, and I'll have it in time to make a decision."

But Duffy felt that the report was beside the point by then. The President's mind was made up. The old hawk's gut reaction was always to fight, and it looked as if he had already decided to move in troops and supplies, and to hell with world opinion.

Duffy remembered how excited de Leon had been, finally able to work outside the usual American intelligence channels. "Perhaps," he had told Duffy, "there is hope for Costa Bella after all."

Duffy ordered another double and paid his bar bill when the drink was delivered. It wouldn't do to get stinko in a Georgetown pub frequented by many members of official Washington. Far better a thing it is I do, Duffy thought, to finish this binge in the privacy of my apartment.

Dr. Willard Lee was exhausted. Traffic had been heavy all the way from Malibu, where he lived, to the mid-Wilshire area, where the Biltmore Hotel was located.

He hadn't been to the Biltmore since the night that Bobby Kennedy was shot there. If it had been up to Dr. Willard Lee he would never have returned.

But this wasn't in his hands.

The Toyota in front of him slammed on the brakes and Dr. Lee almost rear-ended the bright red Japanese sedan. He cursed furiously and leaned on his horn. His head was pounding with a headache that had been unrelenting since early morning. He felt nauseated and dizzy and was running late.

Fifteen minutes later he wheeled his Buick into the Biltmore parking area, jumped out, and thrust the keys at the parking attendant. He checked his wrist-watch and saw that he was already ten minutes late.

What the hell, he thought. They'll stall till I get there. He scowled. When you're the honored guest at one of these things, they can't very well start without you.

He could hear the laughter and the applause as he turned down the corridor leading to the main dining room on the first floor. He paused for a moment out-side the doors to the room and ran a hand through his thinning gray hair. He breathed deeply, swallowed, then adjusted his tie.

Smiling, he entered the dining room just as Dan Fogarty, the master of ceremonies, delivered the punch line of his joke. The gathered guests laughed heartily, more a tribute to the strong drinks served by the bartender than to the newness of Fogarty's jokes.

"Here he is now!" Fogarty exclaimed, obviously relieved that Dr. Lee had shown up. Fogarty led the applause as Dr. Lee made his way to the dais. Dr. Lee shook

hands with acquaintances as he slowly
made his way through the packed tables.
Once on the dais, Fogarty introduced him
formally.

"There's not a one of us who does what
this man does. He's a man who takes his
Hippocratic Oath seriously. We've all read
about his exploits—his many missions of
mercy to our less fortunate neighbors. Who
flew down to the state of Chiapas, in Mexico, during an outbreak of typhoid? Who
helped earthquake victims in Guatemala
with on-the-spot medical relief? And who
is now treating the victims of the Communist led insurrection in Costa Bella? I
don't have to go any further! I give you
Dr. Willard Lee!"

Dr. Willard Lee shook hands with the
florid-faced Dan Fogarty and then acknow-
ledged the cheers of the guests with a wave
of his hand. Dr. Lee, the airborne medic,
was smiling broadly and standing tall.

He wished Barnes were present. It would
be good for a laugh.

When Chet Barnes returned to his office
in Langley, Virginia, he felt wired. He liked
living on the edge, feeling the sharpness
of existence pressing against him. It had
been a close one this time. Luckily, Duffy's man had blown it somehow. He hadn't
reported in time, and that had brought
CIA into it.

Jorge de Leon. Barnes had ordered a check through the military data bank. Now he had the printout in front of him. De Leon was a classic, educated in American military schools, devoted to the ideals of democracy. Just the kind of guy CIA loved to recruit once he returned to his native land.

Barnes wondered how they'd missed him.

No sense worrying about it now. The main thing was to keep the President on track. Barnes didn't know what de Leon had managed to dig up, but Barnes knew that it was going to go no further. There was too much riding on this.

Mr. de Leon was going to be located, all right. And when it was all over, that joker Duffy from the Justice Department was going to wish that he'd never heard the name de Leon.

It took only thirty seconds for Barnes to reach Costa Bella, and another thirty seconds for Colonel Pedro Rojas to be run to ground and put on the line. It was a relatively simple matter. After all, Pedro Rojas was well placed within the Costa Bellan security forces. "His name," Barnes said, "is Jorge de Leon. You might know him."

There was momentary silence on the other end. "I do," Rojas whispered. His voice was enough to chill Chet Barnes.

"Make it look good," Barnes said.

There was a soft laugh. "I think I have the perfect solution," Rojas answered.

"Take him in," Barnes warned, "but go no further. This has to look *very* good."

Then Barnes broke the connection and sat back in his chair. His heart was racing. His mouth was dry. There was one more step to take.

Barnes dialed a number on the red phone and waited until the security scrambler was in effect. He dictated a ten-word message and then gave instructions: place the message in the *Wall Street Journal* classified ads section as quickly as possible, using Agency muscle to speed things up.

Now all he had to do was sit back.

three _____

Gavin saw the knife enter his forearm, deflect off the bone, and come out the other side. The dark-haired man Gavin was fighting with grinned at Gavin and jerked the blade upwards, severing tendons and blood vessels, opening Gavin's arm like badly cleaned fish.

Gavin stepped back and gripped the torn skin of his arm. He felt the power of his jetting blood as it pulsed through his fingers. There was no pain, and that was good. Gavin didn't like pain.

The dark-haired man was circling him, not taking any chances even though his opponent was seriously injured. Gavin nodded, appreciating his tormentor's professionalism. One step at a time. Little by little, no need to rush. No medals for speed. Just do the job right, make the other guy dead before he does it to you. Simple and direct.

Gavin recognized his assailant. It was Barlov, the Russian paymaster. It was strange seeing Barlov here. How did Barlov find him in Colorado? No one except Coletti knew Gavin lived in High Card, Colorado, and Coletti would die before he'd tell anyone.

Gavin looked around the room, suddenly conscious that he was in Kendall's living room, above the bookshop. What was he doing here, fighting for his life with Barlov?

Barlov took him while Gavin was drifting with his thoughts and shoved the seven-inch blade into Gavin's stomach with such force that he knocked the wind out of Gavin's lungs. Gavin felt the sudden loss of breath and the curious new opening at the same time. When Gavin opened his eyes he was on his hands and knees on the floor. When he looked down underneath him he saw a steaming pile of guts that he had every reason to believe were his own.

This didn't make any sense, he thought. Maybe it was the loss of blood. Wasn't that part of his training somewhere? Gavin remembered: loss of blood impairs the functioning of the mind, especially the logical rational processes so important to physical survival.

Barlov was sitting on his back now, playing pony with him. Gavin was disgusted. He too had had to kill men, men he didn't know, men who bore him no harm. But he had never humiliated them like

this, never tormented them in their last
moments on earth.

In fact, he hadn't killed Barlov that way,
so why was Barlov acting like this? He
had shot Barlov between the eyes as the
Russian had sat waiting for a bus in
Amsterdam. And that was two years ago.

Gavin suddenly awoke with a start. He
was shivering, the dream fresh in his mind.
Outside, the village of High Card, Colorado,
was covered with fresh-fallen snow. From
his bedroom window he could see Kendall's
Book Store. Everything was OK.

Teniente Jorge de Leon walked back to
the barracks, his head blurred by half a
bottle of *aquadiente*. His throat was dry
from too many cigarettes. He had put off
making contact because he had yet to figure out a satisfactory way of explaining
his hand in the deaths of the nuns.

He knew it was not of his own doing. He
knew that the final shots from his .45 had
been a mercy. Still, he could not deal with
it.

Inside his small room he quickly undressed and lay down on the narrow bed.
The air outside his window was still,
humid, and hot. He breathed deeply, trying
to sleep, knowing that sleep was not going
to be easy.

He heard them coming for him.

The steady clomp of military boots and

the precise but muffled sounds were familiar to him. The steps grew closer and closer
until he heard them tromp up the barracks
stairs, come down the open area towards
the officers' rooms. Then his door was
thrust open. Rojas stood there, framed in
the light pouring in from the corridor.
"Teniente?" he asked. "On your feet if you
please." Rojas clicked on the overhead light.
The room quickly filled with wide-eyed
recruits clutching their M-14's too tightly.

Rojas walked to the chair where de Leon
had tossed his gun belt. The .45 was still
holstered and Rojas made a show of pick-
ing it up by the buckle—for the edification
of the troops no doubt. "This is yours?" he
asked.

De Leon nodded.

"Please answer," Rojas said, glancing at
the others.

"It's mine," de Leon said in a steady voice.

"Very well." Rojas handed the gun belt
to a gruff, barrel-chested sergeant and
ordered de Leon taken into custody.

This was making no sense at all, de Leon
thought.

four _____

The snow was knee-deep on the path that Gavin usually took into town. Earlier, when he awoke, he had peered from his bedroom window and seen the effects of the night's snowfall. There was no reason to wander down the hill into town, he thought. Plenty of food and drink already stored in the cabin.

Then he had seen the bright red swatch of flannel flagging from Kendall's. Kendall's Book Store was a two-story affair, a wood frame building that housed the book operation on the ground floor, with living quarters above. It fronted on Main Street. The rear of the building faced the wooded foothill on which sat Gavin's cabin.

The bright red cloth flying from the upper window of Kendall's meant that Gavin had mail. The cabin had no phone, so if you wanted Gavin, you left a message with Kendall. Simple and efficient.

Except on a day like this, Gavin thought.

Gavin put a pot of water on to boil,

quickly washed up, and then tugged on a black turtleneck wool sweater, Levi's, and thick cotton socks. He mixed up a cup of coffee, drank it quickly while he brought his blood pressure to a boil with a couple of quickly smoked cigarettes. Then he pulled on a pair of fleece-lined snow boots and a dark blue down parka.

Twenty minutes later he walked in on Kendall in the middle of a big sale. "Five paperbacks, at three for a dollar or forty-nine cents a piece. Listen—why don't you pick out another one? Six or five, it's the same price," Kendall said to the customer.

The customer nodded dumbly. He was a stoned-out student from High Card High looking for enough science fiction to get him through the weekend. "I get another one for the same price?" the student asked.

"If you want," Kendall said. Gavin had never met a person as patient as Kendall. As soon as the student shuffled off towards the sci-fi stacks Kendall turned to Gavin. "Been hiding out up there? I only see you when I show the flag."

Gavin shrugged. "Doing some reading, some sleeping. Nothing much happening. What's the flag for?"

Kendall reached under the counter. "The usual—Monday's *Wall Street Journal,* some junk mail."

Gavin picked up the *Wall Street Journal* and turned to the classifieds.

"Looking for work?" Kendall asked.

Gavin shrugged. "Anything else?"

Kendall handed him a light blue envelope. "Only the gas bill," Kendall said.

Gavin slid the mail into his pocket and stepped back as the student wandered back to the counter. "I found another one," he said, smiling, proud of himself.

Kendall collected the two dollars plus tax and turned to Gavin. "So are you leaving town?"

"Probably."

"Damn. I was going to have a nice little sit-down dinner this Friday. Just a few couples. I wanted you to be there."

"Sorry."

"How about if I move it up to tonight?"

Gavin smiled and shook his head. "Sorry. I'll be on a plane this afternoon."

"Maybe when you get back then," Kendall said.

Gavin took in her long blonde hair and deep blue eyes. "Kendall," he said, "you can depend on it."

Gavin dragged Dorn out from underneath a 1927 Bugatti roadster and asked him if he was doing anything that afternoon. "Aw hell no," Dorn said, wiping his hands on a greasy rag. "What the hell do I have to do except drive you around? I mean, who cares if I ever get through bringing this beauty back to life? Certainly not my creditors, because they all told me, 'Dorn, you can pay us whenever the hell you please.' "

They were in the main workroom of Dorn's auto restoration shop. Two other Bugattis, in various stages of distress, waited their turns. Dorn rubbed his high forehead with the back of his hand. He was a huge man, whose mechanical talent payed the freight on his awesome—and expensive—personal tastes.

"I need a lift to the airport. Denver."

"OK," Dorn said, walking to the office. "Let me clean up. What time do you have to leave? Do we have time for a couple of drinks or what?" Dorn set two glasses on his desk.

"Sure."

Dorn poured out two fingers of Bushmill's Irish Whiskey into each glass, then handed one to Gavin. "Same deal as always?" Dorn said after he sipped his whiskey.

"Sure." Gavin reached into his coat pocket. He took out a plain white envelope stuffed to an unusual thickness. Dorn took it, placed it in the office safe. Then he closed the steel door and spun the tumbler.

"Why do we go through this every time?" Dorn asked. "There's a bank across the street. They'll hold your money too, you know. It's their business. And they'll pay you for the privilege."

"Fuck banks," Gavin said.

* * *

When Gavin's flight touched down at
Kennedy International Airport in New
York City it was 9:10, East Coast time. He
was glad that he had managed to get
through to Coletti from the Denver airport.
Coletti was free that evening. "You can
only stay one night?" Coletti had asked
over the phone. "When are Gina and the
kids going to get a chance to see you?"

Gavin didn't have the time. Two years
ago he'd spent three days with the Colettis
during the final stages of his recupera-
tion from a gunshot wound. Gina Coletti
was the perfect wife and mother as far as
Gavin was concerned: sarcastic and opin-
ionated when the occasion demanded.

As for Coletti, Gavin had met him in
'Nam and they had served together for six
months. That was a long time ago but
every time they met they could still see it
in each other's eyes.

Gavin shuttled in from Kennedy to Grand
Central Station, then took a cab to Green-
wich Village. He told the cabby to stop
near Sheridan Square. He walked the rest
of the way, his mind flooded with memories. New York did that to him. He felt at
once at home but also alienated. There was
no aligning his perceptions into some
smooth illusion.

At Christopher Street he turned right
and walked past apartment buildings lin-

ing the narrow street. Ahead, the lights of Lucia's glowed through the mist.

As soon as Gavin stepped inside the restaurant the warmth and flavor of the place saturated him. The smell was earthy and good and not to be found anywhere in Colorado. There was enough garlic hanging in wreaths from the walls to keep Manhattan free of vampires forever. And in the corner, a bottle of red wine in front of him, sat Nick Coletti. Dressed in a three-piece suit with his tie pulled loose, the top button of his shirt unfastened, Nick Coletti was clearly off-duty, and loving it.

Coletti was on his feet as soon as he saw Gavin. His outstretched arms encircled Gavin and lifted him a half foot off the floor. "Long time," Coletti said. "Too damned long. Why don't you move back here and join the human race? Jesus—you look like Jeremiah Johnson with that damned beard!"

Gavin smiled as he rubbed his hand through his beard, short and well trimmed. "Couldn't Gina make it?" Gavin asked.

Coletti shook his head. "Naw. Bobby's running a temperature and that's that. She's from the old school. The kid's got a fever, no one leaves the house for anything."

They sat down and Coletti poured a glass of wine for Gavin. "I already ordered," Coletti said. "So tell me—you still with the government?"

"This is it," Gavin said, taking a swig from his glass. "Last one. I have a contract and the contract's up. After this one they have to put me out to feed." He smiled. "I'm looking forward to it. Hell, fifteen grand a year is plenty of money for me. That plus what I've got put away."

Coletti was shaking his head. "Some deal," he said. "I've still got a few years to go. I'll only be forty-three when I bust out."

"Come to Colorado and see me when you retire."

"I plan to." Lucia's daughter Nicole arrived with an antipasto, which she placed between them. She was only sixteen and couldn't actually remember Gavin, no matter how much Coletti reminded her that there was a time, when she was about nine years old, when she was in love with Gavin.

As soon as Nicole stepped away from the table Coletti's eyes turned serious. "Ever since you showed up with that hole in you I've been worried."

Gavin smiled. "Don't be. It was my fault. I messed up. My deals are clean when it comes to getting hurt."

Coletti wiped his mouth with his napkin. "Look, I don't know what you're into with the government—and you're not going to tell me. But I know you, and I know how wrong some deals can get."

"You've seen quite a few of those yourself, Nick. Being a homicide investigator can't be a barrel of laughs all the time."

Coletti grinned. "You get used to it," he said. "Maybe I got used to it in 'Nam. As used to it as you can ever get." He shook his head. "You just have to stop asking yourself, 'Why would anyone do something like this?' They do, and that's that. Next question."

"Next question is—what are you so worried about?"

"I'm worried because I've seen how the government operates. I've seen them burn guys for no reason—or no reason that I could see. Sometimes I think there's a whole other world out there, the world where the power really is. It's like the Mob—I bust some wise guy and I know and he knows that he's nothing. The guys pulling the strings can't be touched. Half the time you don't even know who they are. That's what the government seems like to me. A front."

Gavin said, "You're probably right."

five _____

Jack Duffy awoke with a monumental
headache. The headache was part of the
job, of course. You can't get to your mid-
forties and keep the same drinking habits
you had as a young man. Doesn't work.

He sat up groaning. He supported himself on stiff arms, palms flat against the
mattress. It wasn't worth it. He was going
to have to find another way of playing the
game.

It was a hard habit to break. Government work carries with it social obliga-
tions, and Jack Duffy had tried very hard
to be obliging. He was single, and therefore a much sought-after dinner guest.

A glance at the bedside clock was all
Duffy needed. He heaved himself out of
bed, got to the bathroom, and had the
shower running before he had to sit down
again.

Damn, he thought. Just what the hell
did I have to drink last night? Scotch most
of the time, he was sure of it. Maybe a

little wine with dinner, some cognac to chase it all down. Manhattans later on? He was fuzzy on details. He stood up and got under the hot spray, then belatedly peeled off his wet shorts. He tossed them onto the bathroom floor.

A mistake any man could make.

Later as he dressed, he realized that his drinking was getting out of hand. Nothing much by Washington standards, of course, but that was only because damned near everyone in government was an alcoholic.

He was feeling the effects of the booze. It didn't feel good. Plus, he wasn't enjoying himself at all. Things were worse than ever at the department, and that was a lot of his concern.

He smiled and shook his head as he knotted his striped tie in a thick, unfashionable knot. Young men can afford to be mavericks but older ones can't. He'd been his own man for too long, never willing to kiss the right ass or ball the right wife. Traits like that can cripple a man's career.

Jack Duffy was lucky. He worked because he wanted to. He worked in the Justice Department because it was important work for a man to do.

But he'd made many enemies because of his logical mind, his desire to punish wrongdoers, and his inability to understand why certain criminals weren't nailed just because they were members of the same government he was.

He shook his head. He knew that he had to telephone Marianne to apologize for making an ass of himself. She was a wonderful woman. He should have married her years ago. But he missed the moment and didn't know how to get back to it.

He cleared his mind of his personal life to focus on the pending operations of the day. He was due for a report on de Leon today. That was a report he was eagerly awaiting.

Barnes had told Duffy that CIA would have something by midday.

Duffy checked the time—9:45. He'd just make it if he didn't run into any horrendous traffic.

At 9:56 flight 102 from New York City settled onto the tarmac of Dulles just outside Washington, D.C. Gavin gripped his pack. He was first in line facing the rear exit as the flight attendant turned and announced that they would be exiting forward. So Gavin became last in line.

The Washington air was brisk but the sun was out. It was just what Gavin needed.

It felt good. He felt good. This was his last trip to Washington—ever—and he wanted to sign off on a good note.

He taxied to the Sheraton near the airport, checked in, then showered. He left a wake-up call for twelve noon. The room was quiet. Heavy drapes cut out the light. He slept soundly and awoke, refreshed, with the ringing telephone.

Gavin clipped his beard down to a stubble before he broke out his Rolls razor, the type his father had preferred. A single blade encased in a metal housing resembling a silver cigarette case—the sides of which provided both the stone and the strop needed to sharpen the blade. A handle was lodged in the case as well. He lathered his face and shaved his tender skin carefully. When he was through, he rubbed witch hazel on, his eyes smarting from the sting.

Outside of pale cheeks and jaw he was presentable. His gray eyes were flecked with red. His gaunt cheeks gave him a youthful look, but the lines around his mouth and the set of his jaw offset any hint of boyishness. His muscle tone, he saw, was good—better than he deserved, considering the physical abuse in his life.

There was no sense putting too fine a point on it. He looked like he was thirty-four years old, and while he wasn't getting better looking with age he wasn't turning into a cartoon either. Gavin dug through his pack. He pulled out the double-knit blue blazer and the gray slacks, along with his one white dress shirt, a subdued maroon tie, and a pair of black slip-ons.

Gavin smiled as he dressed in the uncomfortable but always neat double-knits. Somewhere in Washington, in a storage locker that he'd been paying for all these years, were a few suitcases containing all those Brooks Brothers and J. Press wool suits, summer suits, sports coats, and the like. Those were the days when he thought Washington was a big deal. He had dressed like he belonged and damned if everyone didn't believe him.

But it had gotten too heavy, nice suits and all. He had tried to quit. But they reminded him that he had a contract. They didn't like people who wanted out on a contract. They told him how he could go back in the military if he reneged on his deal. They told him how they could furnish a small cell in Leavenworth where he could appeal his court-martial in pure prison comfort.

So he compromised. He would do his end of the deal but he would do it on his own terms. When they had an assignment they could always reach him. He would do what they said. But he wasn't going to sit around in an office at the Department of Agriculture and pretend to be studying the corn price support program just to make the whole stinking deal look good.

Barnes had smiled and said that it sounded all right to him. Barnes told him that he thought all that cover was stupid any-

way. Gavin didn't have to pretend to be a
Washington bureaucrat if he didn't want
to, Barnes had said. Go play somewhere.
Just let us know where you are. We'll be
in touch.

It was very simple. When they said kill,
Gavin killed. He had a contract for eight
assignments, and this one would be number eight.

six _____

Jorge de Leon knew he was a dead man.

The thought of his impending death made him uneasy—nothing else. It was a factor he had lived with for years. He had seen others die, and he had realized that sooner or later his turn would come.

The cell in which he sat was flat gray in color, about ten feet by ten feet. In the corner was a hole in the floor which served as his latrine. The door was solid steel with a porthole of reinforced glass. There were no windows, just a ceiling vent.

Outside sounds did not reach him, and that was the most terrifying thing of all. He had never been in so secure an area. Escape was impossible. He would die and he knew it.

They had left him cigarettes. He smoked one after the other. He ran a hand through his hair as he sat on the edge of his bunk and realized that it had all been a matter of coincidence, bad timing, or whatever other name a man could give the final game.

41

So stupid, really. A death in battle was far preferable to this.

That first night had been the worst. "Accompany me, if you please," Rojas had said, "because there is something I think you should see."

De Leon had no choice. The silent soldier beside Rojas had thrust his rifle into de Leon's guts, doubling him over with crushing pain. He staggered after Rojas, who kept up a mindless chatter as they made their way down an endless hall towards the sound of someone screaming.

Rojas opened the door and pushed de Leon in. Strapped to an operating table was a man of about his age, de Leon noticed. The man—his fearful eyes wide with pain and hopelessness—had barely noticed the appearance of de Leon and Rojas.

All of his attention was on the man dressed as a surgeon, a scalpel in his hand, who stood beside the operating table.

"Excuse me, colonel," the white-clad figure said to Rojas. "I was just playing with him. I've saved the actual operation until you came."

"Splendid," Rojas said, and de Leon saw that Rojas's smile appeared to be genuine. He really was pleased that the massacre had been delayed for his pleasure.

Slowly, and with no skill, the white-clad figure made an incision from the man's

collarbone to his pubis. The scream was
unlike anything de Leon had ever heard.
As the blood pulsed from the long, narrow
wound Rojas stepped closer, to see it better.

"If you please." Rojas held out his hand
and the white-clad figure—de Leon doubted
that he was a medical doctor—handed the
instrument to Rojas.

Rojas turned and grinned at de Leon—a
grin of happy, childlike pleasure. "Come
closer," he said to de Leon, and the rifle
butt in his kidney insured de Leon's prompt
response.

Rojas made another incision, this one
even more amateurish and heavy-handed
than the other. The victim's vocal chords
had become paralyzed with shock. His
neck, thick with the strain, was vibrating.
His eyes had rolled back into his head and
the sound of his breathing was the only
sound that de Leon was conscious of.

"And now?" Rojas sounded like a student doing an experiment.

"Now," said the white-clad figure, "I
believe we simply tug the skin open."

It was messy work but they did it. De
Leon glanced down into the bloody, pul-
sating chest cavity and felt the bile rising
in his throat as Rojas began to finger the
beating heart, laughing in a high-pitched
voice as he did so. "It tickles!" he said,
turning to his fellow monster. "Try it—very
interesting!"

That was when de Leon passed out.

Later, Rojas had dropped by de Leon's cell and told him that he had nothing to worry about. "As a member of the armed forces," Rojas told de Leon, "it is unthinkable that we would treat you that way." Then he laughed.

De Leon knew at least that he would go to his death revealing nothing. Not because they didn't possess the means to force him to talk—not at all. It was just that he didn't know anything, so no matter how much they tortured him, they would get nothing.

His contact? Certainly, *capitán*. A middle-aged man, a bit overweight. American, of course. The air of Washington to him, that studied nonchalance everyone who dealt with American foreign service officers understood.

His name? Here de Leon would have to smile, and if he could manage it, to laugh. The contact's name would be meaningless. The name the chubby Americano used was Flynn. Errol Flynn? Or was it Wayne? Or Redford? Or Disney? In any case it wasn't his real name and the *capitán* would certainly understand that.

But they would torture him nonetheless, perhaps for the sheer fun of it. De Leon had been witness to sessions of physical interrogation. He felt a wave of heat in his stomach as he thought of them.

When they were through with him, or

what was left of him, they would turn him over to an executioner and de Leon's misery would be at an end.

It was the way many Costa Bellans died.

It was a shame, really. There was no question about the situation in Costa Bella. Going out in the field had been an indulgence. He didn't have to leave Bahia, the capital, to tell the *americanos* what was going on. But they had required eyewitness verification, and he had agreed to give it to them.

And now this. The blood of four innocents on his hands—that is how it would look in the press. Nothing he could say would change the fact that his .45 was involved. So anything else he had to say would be dismissed.

Jorge de Leon lighted another cigarette from the one he was smoking.

It was only a matter of time now. He hoped the man that they sent was professional. He wanted it over with as quickly as possible.

Barnes said, "This one is going to be easy."

"None of them are easy. 'Easy' exists in the minds of guys like you who just plan things. Everything's easy from that desk. Try it once for real. Then tell me about easy."

Barnes tossed the folder atop his desk.

"Gavin," he said, "I've never liked you. I've always thought you should have been returned to the military. Sometimes I get the impression that you don't take this very seriously."

"The way this job was explained to me, I come here and you tell me who to kill and I kill. Take your impressions to the Agency shrink."

Barnes stood up. He liked to stand as straight as possible, Gavin had noticed, probably because Barnes came in at maybe five-foot four. Gavin checked Barnes' shoes. A bit extra in the heels as well. Barnes wore glasses and kept his hair length to about three millimeters. He had the stocky, solid shape of a middle-aged jogger who keeps checking his pulse as he clicks off the K's.

"This is the last one, isn't it?" Barnes asked.

Gavin smiled, Barnes knew as well as he did that this was the last one. You make a contract for eight kills, then number eight is the last one. Gavin didn't answer him.

"Too bad it couldn't be a difficult one. Those are the ones you prefer, aren't they? The kills wherein the victim is armed, and usually knows you're coming. You like to kill the ones who are trying to kill you."

Gavin said nothing.

"I think that's stupid. It's certainly inefficient. You should want the sure things in life, Gavin. Take the odds whenever you can."

"So that I'll grow up and be like you?"

Barnes stiffened—Gavin made it another full quarter inch of height. He should stay pissed all the time, Gavin thought. He'd be taller.

Barnes slowly took his seat behind the desk. He opened the folder that sat on the desktop. Then he glanced up at Gavin.

"I suppose it's time to get down to business." His eyes held Gavin's steadily. "Tell me, Gavin. Here in the Agency you are known as a Terminator. We have a group of them, you know. But I've always felt that with you there was a touch of the mercenary. The other men are more dedicated, it seems. Believers. You don't believe in any of it, Gavin."

"I have to believe in some things. I believe that this is my last assignment, and that afterwards you and your people have no hold on me."

Barnes chuckled. "As well you should, Gavin. We keep our word."

Gavin said nothing.

Barnes sighed. "His name is de Leon," Barnes said. "Perhaps you read about him in the morning edition of the *Post*."

"Costa Bella? The murder of the four missionaries?"

"Same man. The Costa Bellan authori-

ties don't know what to do with him. He
must be taken out. There's too much media
attention being paid to the entire affair.
The attention is getting in the way of more
serious operations. The Costa Bellan Government has a revolution on its hands. It
wants this thing settled quickly."

"So why import an American to do it?
Why not let them handle it themselves?
Surely they've got someone who can do
the job. Besides, the guy's in custody—a
sitting duck."

"That's exactly the problem. They don't
want to appear to be covering up, which is
exactly the way the press would play it if
de Leon turned up dead while in custody.
The press would say that obviously de Leon
was killed to prevent him from talking,
from implicating other members of the
government's security forces, or even perhaps members of the government itself."
Barnes shook his head. "Just won't do. As
you know, Costa Bella is essential to our
government's foreign policy in the Central
American region. We have a stake in the
government of Costa Bella. We have trea-
ties and we have friends there."

"You don't have to sell me, Barnes."

"Good. I've arranged your passage on a
commercial jet leaving Dulles at 4:30 this
afternoon." He handed Gavin an oversized
envelope. "It's all there. Passport, tickets,
liaison at the Embassy. Your contact with

the government there will be a Colonel
Rojas. Good man. He'll set it up for you."

Gavin tucked the envelope into his inside
coat pocket. He stood up and walked to the
door.

"I don't suppose I'll be seeing you again,"
Barnes said.

Gavin turned. "You never can tell. It's a
small world," Gavin replied. "But we can
hope."

Duffy was on his fourth cup of coffee.
The *Washington Post* was spread out on
front of him on his desk. He looked glum.

In front of him was a two-column spread
on de Leon's arrest in connection with the
massacre of the missionaries. A small
grainy photo of de Leon, grinning and
holding his rifle in the air, completed the
image of a lunatic Latin American.

Duffy picked up the telephone and punch-
ed in his secretary. "Book me on a flight
to Bahia, Costa Bella," he said. "As quickly
as possible. Let's keep it very quiet."

Then he called his bank and arranged
for three thousand dollars in traveler's
checks. This was going to be an unofficial
visit. He didn't have time to procure department travel funds, and besides, he
didn't want word to get out that he was
going to Costa Bella.

He sat back in his chair and thrust one
foot against his desk. He fished in his

shirt pocket for his cigarettes, realized that they were lost in the jumble of papers on his desk, finally found them and lit one up. He inhaled deeply, his eyes glazed as he tried to figure out what the hell he was going to do once he got to Costa Bella.

There was no doubt that de Leon had been framed. Of course, de Leon had to take some part in the operation, but it was probably done under duress. No matter. They had him cold. He was totally discredited as an informant. But Duffy felt an obligation to the man. It was Duffy who had involved de Leon, and it seemed like the least he could do was to stick by his man now. Duffy cursed the President's decision to bring in CIA to find de Leon. That was where the trouble lay. The Agency was a sieve, and any information CIA had, everyone had.

De Leon was a dead man as soon as the agency got involved. Duffy stubbed out his cigarette angrily. The phone buzzed. He picked it up. Theresa, his secretary, had already booked Duffy on a flight that night. She had made reservations at a new hotel in Bahia. "It's supposed to be terrific," Theresa said. "Eight stories high. The tallest building in the country."

Duffy smiled.

The warm air of Costa Bella washed over Gavin as he stepped out of the 747, walked down the steps and onto the tarmac. It was eighty-eight degrees at eleven o'clock at night. The air was so humid Gavin felt as if he were breathing steam.

Inside the customs-and-immigration shed, uniformed officials passed him through without a hassle. Americans were welcome, and that was that.

Gavin saw his Embassy contact immediately. Clad in a natural shoulder seersucker suit, wearing a tie and clumsy black shoes, he was unmistakably an American. An official one at that. He recognized Gavin and walked over to him.

His name was Hadley. He was the new guy at the Embassy, in charge of greeting visiting firemen, securing hotel reservations, wining and dining VIPs, and other pressing duties. Gavin had met many others like Hadley: eager to please, eager to advance, eager to excel.

"I've taken care of everything," Hadley said. He grinned at Gavin but there was a sharp look to the eyes. "First time in Bahia? Helluva little place. Anything goes, of course, though I can't really take you to some of the more outrageous places. Embassy wouldn't care for it. Could give you some names, though, if you feel like it."

Gavin smiled right back. "Sure," he said. "Let's have those names. Underage girls are my special thing."

Hadley blanched. He swallowed, then brought back the grin. "Well, Mr. Gavin—I guess I put my foot in it that time. You know how it is. I've got to meet everyone who's got any connection at all with the Embassy. Some pretty strange people fill that bill. I guess I just thought that you would like to sample some of Bahia's well-known nighttime activities. But I can see that you are a well-traveled guy. Nothing new for you here," Hadley said.

Gavin said nothing.

"I don't know who it is you're supposed to see at the Embassy," Hadley said in a rush. "Or else I'd have made an appointment for you. But I did make reservations at the Florida—newest hotel in all of Central America. Tallest building in the country!"

Gavin studied him. Hadley kept grinning, though he shifted his weight from one foot to the other. "Where'd you go to school?" Gavin asked.

"Georgetown," Hadley answered brightly. "Master's in international relations."

"Great," Gavin answered. He handed Hadley his claim tickets. "Pick up my luggage, will you? I'll wait here."

It was worth it if only for the look on Hadley's face. That, plus the fact that Gavin's calculated rudeness would insure that Hadley would go out of his way not to string along with Gavin.

Gavin had already secured a taxi by the time Hadley returned, out of breath, with the one piece of luggage that Gavin had brought.

"Thanks," Gavin said. He handed the luggage to the cab driver, who stowed it in the trunk. "What was the name of that hotel again?"

"La Florida," Hadley replied brightly.

"Thanks again," Gavin said, and got into the cab. The driver revved the engine twice, then squealed away from the terminal.

Gavin looked back and saw Hadley standing there, his long arms hanging by his sides. Some days are like that, Gavin thought. Hadley might as well learn that now.

It was a twelve-mile drive into Bahia. Gavin couldn't see much in the darkness. But what he could see reminded him of the Yucatán—flat land covered with scrub, easy enough to get lost in.

Bahia itself was a port city, alive with

commerce, drugs, whores, booze, and good food. It was all jammed into crowded, narrow streets—except by the waterfront. There, the Malecon, the beach-front boulevard, was a broad avenue with the city's major arteries feeding into it. Ships from a dozen countries were unloading. The dock area, even at midnight, was feverish with activity.

The Hotel La Florida was located two blocks from the waterfront. From Gavin's top-floor window he commanded a perfect view of the sea and the commercial traffic that it bore.

He unpacked carefully, letting the exhaustion of the day's journey take him down slowly. He wanted a good night's sleep. It was his experience that a certain amount of time was going to have to be spent in unwinding. He poured a double shot of Jack Daniels in a bathroom glass that had been wrapped in tissue and sterilized. By the time he was through unpacking and through another double Jack, he was ready for bed.

As he lay in bed, de Leon's face floated in his mind. He hadn't said anything to Barnes because he didn't want to give him any sadistic satisfaction. Barnes would have loved knowing that Gavin's last assignment would be his hardest. Gavin slept soundly, disturbed only once by a dream. The dream was lifelike and detailed and so

vivid that when Gavin awoke he had to
force himself to remember that it was only
a dream.

In his dream he had taken Kendall to
dinner. It had been fantastic, as only a
dream can be. The thickest, juiciest steaks
had been consumed, along with two bot-
tles of rare Burgundy. Afterwards, as they
trekked through the snow to Kendall's
place above the bookstore, he had told her
what he had been doing for years. He told
her of the men he had killed, and that the
name she knew him by—Evans—wasn't his
name at all.

When they entered Kendall's living room
she had made for the coffee table and
picked something up. When she turned
around, Gavin saw that it was a .38 Police
Special. It was pointed directly at him.

Kendall told him that he had been lied
to as well. Her name wasn't Kendall. She
had been killing people too.

Only she had one more assignment to go,
and Gavin was it. He could see the tears in
her eyes. She didn't want to do it, she
said, but he was a professional. He understood how it was.

Gavin opened his mouth to speak just as
the barrel of the .38 emitted a red flash.
He felt the thick thud of the slug take him
at the waist. Then Kendall saw that he
was in pain. As he looked up from the
floor through a sudden pink haze he saw

her walking towards him and pulling back
the hammer and telling him to close his
eyes—

And he awoke.

He was breathing hard. He lay still for a
few moments, then got out of bed. He
showered, taking alternate bursts of warm
and cold water, until, refreshed and awake,
he stepped from the stall and toweled dry.

The dream was fading as he dressed and
planned his day. A stop at the Embassy to
make sure all signals were go. There would
be a message from Barnes on that. A meeting with Colonel Rojas, who was supposed
to set up the deal.

That was it.

He dressed in light blue chinos, a pull-
over shirt, and a pair of beat-up deck shoes.

Downstairs in the lobby, Gavin saw that
the civil war, and the massacre, had attracted the cream of the world's press. All
three networks were there, with equipment
and cables making an obstacle course of
the lobby itself. The bar—just off the front
desk—was already boisterous with newsmen drinking breakfast. Outside, the curb
was solid with press vehicles and staff cars
from embassies, international organizations, Costa Bellan Government officials,
and others.

Bahia had never been busier.

As Gavin threaded his way down narrow streets teeming with pedestrians, he

saw that the commercial boom—fruits of war—was very much in evidence. Sidewalk stalls filled with merchandise ranging from fresh fruit and vegetables to Adidas running shoes and Jordache jeans were doing a brisk business. Armed soldiers patrolled with their automatic rifles slung carelessly on their shoulders. Ahead, the gleaming gold eagle perched atop the American Embassy served as a landmark to Gavin as he sauntered easily through the crowd.

Once past the marine guard and into the quiet and clean Embassy grounds, Gavin made straight for the office of Doug Layton, the Embassy's officer for protection and welfare—the Embassy department that aids tourists who have lost their visas or need a doctor or have spent all of their money and can't get home.

Layton was a CIA agent of long standing. Gavin knew him from Gavin's brief spell working in Washington. As he entered Layton's office, the gray-haired, lanky agent stood to shake his hand.

"Good to see you," Layton said. "Don't look too different. How long's it been? Five years?"

Gavin smiled. "Just about," he said. He sat down opposite Layton and lit a cigarette. "How've you been?"

Layton shrugged. "Can't complain. There's worse places to be posted. Lots of action here. Hell, you're here—so you know there's lots of action."

Gavin smiled. "I'm here for clearance," Gavin said.

Layton nodded. "It arrived this morning. Whatever operation you're on, it's go."

Gavin nodded. Suddenly the door to Layton's office opened. A stocky, moon-faced man strode in. "I hear you're the man I've got to see," he said. He glanced at Gavin. "I can wait till you're through."

Layton's face was beginning to redden with supressed anger. "I don't know who you are, mister, but I'll see you when I damn well please. Now get the hell out of my office!"

The stocky, moon-faced man grinned. "Yeah—I guess I am a little out of line. I'll wait outside."

When he closed the door, Gavin turned to Layton. "Busy place," he said.

Layton shook his head. "Some asshole whose wife's probably got a case of the trots and he doesn't trust any of the local medicos. Sometimes I wish I didn't need a cover job for these assignments—or at least one that didn't bring me into contact with the Great Unwashed."

Gavin laughed, then stood up. "I don't need to take up any more of your time," he said to Layton. "I don't guess I'll see you again—I'll be in and out, as they say."

They shook hands. Layton's eyes were steady. "Good luck," he said quietly.

"Thanks," Gavin said.

Outside Layton's office the stocky, moon-faced man grinned at Gavin when Gavin walked by. "Think he's free now?" the man asked.

"Beats me," Gavin said, and continued out of the Embassy. He arrived back at the Hotel La Florida fifteen minutes later. He checked his room carefully but noted nothing out of the ordinary. His luggage had not been searched, nor had the dresser drawers been opened.

So far, so good.

It took twenty minutes on the phone to run down Colonel Rojas at Military Headquarters. "You've been expecting me," Gavin said to Rojas. "My magazine has contacted you about an article I'm doing. I was told you could be of help."

"But of course," Rojas said. Gavin didn't like his voice. Oily and cold. "Can you come by my office? That would be a great help."

"Of course. When would be a good time?"

"After the crush of daily business," Rojas replied smoothly. "Let us say—seven o'clock this evening?"

"I'll be there," Gavin said, and hung up. He didn't like this operation a bit. He didn't like working through officials who might have a stake in the outcome of the hit. He didn't trust them.

It was still early. Gavin took off his clothing, already sweaty from his walk through Bahia. He showered, then decided to rest till the afternoon heat lifted.

Doug Layton stood up and stretched. He felt older than dirt. This job, he thought, might be the last one. He was getting too old for all the deceit and treachery, the outright bloodiness of it all.

He tugged on his lightweight suit jacket and wondered why he bothered with it at all. Of course he knew the reason. He was a ranking Embassy officer and damn it, it didn't matter if it was a hundred and fifty degrees in the shade and so goddamn humid that your socks were wet. You wore a suit and a tie and you tried to look like you didn't mind.

Layton said goodnight to Eva, his Costa Bellan secretary, then signed out at the security desk manned day and night by the marines.

Outside, the muggy air was so thick with motor exhausts and the aroma of uncollected garbage that Layton wanted to turn around and go back inside. But he struggled on to the corner. He paused to wipe the greasy residue from his eyeglasses, and crossed the street.

The appearance of Gavin had been upset-

ting. He had been around long enough to
know that Gavin was reputedly one of the
Terminators. They always made life tough
for the Embassy. There were always too
many questions after men like Gavin showed
up. People started dying, and no one had
any answers. As if that wasn't enough,
the moon-faced man, Duffy, was another
complication. He was Justice Department
all right, because Layton had checked him
out. Layton would have to wait till morning to run down the other details of Duffy's story. First thing, he'd have to contact
the locals and tell them it was strictly
hands off de Leon till Duffy got through
with him. That is, if Duffy's story checked
out. If it didn't—if Duffy was some kind of
wise-ass junior jive out to have a good
time by acting important, Layton was
going to show him just how upset he could
get when someone rattled his cage.

He was standing on the corner of a busy
intersection, lost in thought. It was where
he always waited for a cab. He wasn't conscious of the small, thin young man who
squeezed through the crowd and came in
just behind Layton. He wasn't even really
conscious of the big, green 1949 Buick
that was hurtling down the inside lane,
eight inches from the curb upon which he
stood. A big car being recklessly driven
was not something out of the ordinary in
Bahia, rather it was more the rule.

He yelled "Hey!" when the small hand pressed firmly into his back and pushed him off the curb. Layton stumbled once and looked to his left. He saw the massive green Buick leaping towards him. Then there was a painless impact that he actually thought was kind of funny, and a weightless flight upside down. Then a sudden jolting blackness out of which Doug Layton never came.

When Gavin awoke it was but five-forty-five. He could lie there no longer! Gavin showered again. He dressed in a fresh shirt and pants. He went down to the lobby, turned his room key in at the front desk, then decided to have a beer.

The bar was jammed.

Media types from around the world clogged the bar and booths. There was Parker from the "Nightly News," and Jamison, whose daily column ran in over five hundred papers. There were others Gavin recognized, but it all came to the same thing: the de Leon story was going to be a super media event. Which meant that the kill was going to be covered in detail. Which meant that Gavin had to do it right.

There was a small table in the back of the room that was empty. Gavin headed for it. He slid in just as the waitress arrived. *"Cerveza,"* he said.

"De cual?" she asked. Probably wanted

to know which beer he wanted, but Gavin
was all out of Spanish.

"Doesn't matter," he said in English.

She nodded, scribbled on her pad and
set off for the bar.

"Mind if I join you?"

Gavin looked up. It was the moon-faced
man who'd barged into Layton's office at
the Embassy. "I don't mean to be pushy,"
the man said, "but we almost know each
other and besides, there's not another seat
in the joint."

"Sure," Gavin said. "Have a seat."

The man sat down with a sigh of relief,
then stuck out his hand. "Duffy," he said.

"Gavin," Gavin replied, shaking his hand.
The waitress arrived with two beers.

"I took the liberty of putting these on
my bill," Duffy said.

"Thank you," Gavin said, pouring his
beer—dark and thick—into the tall glass.

They both sipped, glanced around the
room, then realized there was nothing to
do but talk. "Hope you concluded your
business with Layton today," Duffy finally
said.

There was something in his tone that
piqued Gavin's attention. "Sure," he replied.
"Silly thing, really. Just checking for a
nephew of mine about a student visa. Kid
wants to come to Costa Bella and learn
Spanish."

Duffy nodded, not believing a word of it. "Layton was killed today," he said.

Gavin stared at him. "What?"

Duffy took a sip of beer. "About an hour ago. Left the Embassy to go home—hit and run. Happened about two blocks from the Embassy."

Gavin swallowed more beer. "That's a shock," he said. His mind was racing. Layton was his only official contact in Costa Bella. Rojas couldn't be trusted—he wasn't with the Agency.

"Yeah," Duffy said. "I didn't have much luck with him. He finally threw me out of his office." Duffy shrugged.

"They didn't find the driver?"

"Not as far as I know." Duffy studied Gavin closely, then glanced around at the other tables before speaking. "I'm with the Justice Department," Duffy said. "I had some business with Layton."

Gavin nodded. "So?"

Duffy smiled. "Without getting into the details, let's just say that I'm wondering if your business with Layton touched on mine."

Gavin smiled. "I doubt it," he said. "Unless you've got a nephew who wants to learn Spanish."

This time Duffy grinned. "Why come so far to learn Spanish? Mexico's a lot closer, isn't it? Lot safer too. And you had to fly all the way down here to talk to Layton about it?"

Gavin laughed. "That's the story," he said. "I don't really see why I have to convince you of anything. Still, if you feel like talking, it's fine with me. You bought the beer."

Duffy sighed as he sat back. "Yeah, and I'm going to buy a few more of 'em before the day's out. First Layton, then Rojas. What a combo."

Gavin's eyes betrayed nothing. "Someone else get killed too? Rojas?"

Duffy shook his head. "No. I went to see him on business—he's head of security for Bahia when he's in the capital."

Gavin finished his beer. "Got to go," he said to Duffy. "Hope things work out for you."

Duffy raised his glass in salute. "Say hello to Rojas for me," Duffy said.

This time Gavin's reactions weren't fast enough, and the piercing glance he directed at Duffy gave it away.

"Maybe we'll talk again," Gavin said.

Duffy smiled. "I hope so," he answered.

Dr. Willard Lee prepared a greasy ball of opium slowly, forming it gently in his hand. The room was small, quiet, and utterly comfortable. He reclined on soft cushions, resting on his side, smiling.

His bony body was concealed by a long,

warm robe, which reached the floor. As he lighted his pinioned ball and drew deeply, he relaxed, letting his mind fold in on itself like a flower blossoming in reverse. His eyes closed as the warm, sensual feeling expanded.

Three days to go.

One more mission.

And then he was home free.

Dr. Willard Lee put down the pipe. He trembled on the edge of unconsciousness, the near void to which he was so attracted. For a few moments no one was home, and Dr. Willard Lee was nothing more than a sensing device operated by a set of automated motor controls, all wheels spinning, going nowhere. Gradually he was conscious of himself again, memories, desires, and sense impressions of the present once again cluttering his mind.

Dr. Lee sighed softly. He felt it more than he used to. He knew what it was doing to his health. He tried to make up for the damage by eating correctly and keeping himself dosed with multivitamins, but in the end it didn't seem to matter. He was beginning to look like the others that he could remember in the pleasure houses of Bangkok and Saigon.

He sat up and pressed his palm over his suddenly hot, wet forehead. Dr. Willard Lee wanted nothing to go wrong on this last trip. He wanted no foul-ups, nothing

out of the ordinary. He knew what it was—
the normal, plain desire to get it over with,
not to be one of those all-time losers who
blow it on the last mission: the dogface
who eats a land mine on his last day of
combat duty; the fly-boy on his last flight
ejecting with the canopy still in place. Dr.
Willard Lee knew that there was a cruel
game going on for guys who had to do it
just *one more time.*

Dr. Lee didn't want to play.

When the telephone rang, a few hours
later, Dr. Lee was wearing a dark gray
business suit, fresh from the dry cleaners.

In a half hour he was due at the Madi-
gans', which was the beginning of the
social whirl that always kicked off a Mission of Mercy.

Everyone wanted to shake the good doctor's hand and have a photograph taken
with him.

Dr. Lee picked up the telephone on the
second ring. He recognized Barnes' raspy
voice at once. "It's ready," the voice said.
"Good luck."

The doctor hung up the receiver. He
stared at himself in the mirrored grandfa-
ther clock beside the telephone. One more
time. Just one more time.

eight _____

By the time Gavin arrived at the offices of
National Security, a gray colonial building located near the main plaza of Bahia,
the air had cooled to a muggy ninety
degrees. The evening was just about to
begin for the inhabitants of Bahia. The
city didn't come to life until nightfall, but
then it was nonstop till two or three in the
morning. Many restaurants were their
busiest at midnight. Considering the day-
time heat, it was easy to understand why.

Two soldiers in starched uniforms stood
at attention, armed with assault rifles. A
third stepped toward Gavin from inside
the building and asked for his identification in a pleasant enough manner.

Minutes later Gavin was escorted to the
private office of Colonel Rojas.

The man who stood up and walked around
his desk to shake Gavin's hand was in his
mid-thirties, perfectly groomed, in obvious
peak physical condition. He smiled easily,
flashing even white teeth at Gavin. He wore

no cologne, nor did he have hair gleaming
with scented oil. His eyes were cold and
dead when he looked at Gavin directly.

"A drink? Coffee?"

"No thanks," Gavin said. "Just tell me
the story, and I'll be on my way."

Rojas nodded his head. "Quite simple.
De Leon is a beast, of course—his crime
testifies to that. However, there are political considerations here. We must not appear to be covering up, you understand—"

Gavin interrupted. "How am I going to
do it?"

Rojas sat up straight. "Ah. That will be
simplicity itself. We shall release him. You
shall kill him."

Now it was Gavin who spoke quickly.
"Release him? You're going to turn de Leon
loose after busting him for the murder of
four innocent people? Religious ones at
that?"

Rojas was grinning. "We are a law-abid-
ing democracy," he said. "Much like your
own. The evidence against de Leon is not
as conclusive as we first thought. The bal-
listics tests are invalid. The witnesses are
not available. In short, he shall be released,
and then you shall kill him."

Gavin thought he had never heard such
a load of pure bullshit in his life. His other
seven hits had seemed like pure acts of
justice compared to this one. Gavin didn't
know what the point of it was. He still

couldn't figure out why they hadn't blown away de Leon as soon as they caught him and spared everyone the trouble.

It figured that his last hit would be such a goddamned mess.

"So where will he be released? Give me a time and a place. Will he be armed?"

Rojas grinned. "He will be armed, of course. His sidearm will be returned to him when he is released. His release will occur at eleven o'clock this evening. It will be done quietly. After all, it would be a matter of prime concern to the various journalists to interview de Leon, and we cannot have that. A fabricated interview is being prepared. It will be distributed to various journalists who will, for a fee, state that they were present for his release."

Gavin nodded. It was obvious now. De Leon knew something—or Rojas thought de Leon knew something—and that was why he was being killed.

Bury all the bullshit about the nuns and the priest, Gavin thought. It was this other thing that meant de Leon was going to die.

Gavin remembered his meeting with Barnes. He hadn't wanted to give Barnes anything to delight himself with, so he withheld a piece of information from him.

It wouldn't have changed anything. Gavin would still have been assigned to terminate de Leon, only it would have given

Barnes a touch of pleasure to know that de Leon was no stranger to Gavin.

The two men had taken advanced training together at Fort Sill ten summers before. They had grown to know each other pretty well.

De Leon would see him coming and know what it was all about.

Gavin wondered what de Leon would do.

Rojas was writing on a note pad. He glanced up at Gavin and smiled. "He will walk out of here at eleven," Rojas said again. "There is nothing more to say."

Gavin stood. "There is one thing," he said.

"Yes?"

"I believe I am to be provided with a weapon."

"Yes—of course," Rojas answered, sliding open a desk drawer. "Here it it. What you prefer, I believe."

Gavin took the .45 automatic and checked it out. He turned and left the room after stuffing the automatic in his attaché case. Gavin walked back to the Hotel La Florida still puzzled by the odd notes of his assignment.

He had killed Barlov the Russian paymaster in France. That had screwed up payments to agents, and among the cost-conscious French that act had been enough to dismantle the Soviet intelligence apparatus for months.

There had been even more of a reason to eliminate Cortez, a Cuban agent working out of southern Florida. He had been one of the reasons the Bay of Pigs had been such an expensive disaster for the United States. He paid dearly for the information he relayed to his superiors in Havana. There were all the others, men who had to be killed, and killed quickly.

Now there was de Leon.

What the hell were they so worried about? What did they think de Leon knew that made his death so important?

As Gavin entered La Florida's lobby he was once again struck by the international attention events in Costa Bella were attracting. The foreign press was represented in almost as many numbers as the American press. The war in Costa Bella was being seen as another test of the American will to fight. Would the United States back the Costa Bellan Government? Was it another Vietnam? Did the Americans have the will to win?

To Gavin, the answers were obvious. Once upon a time a man was expected to defend his home and his country. That meant not leaving his home or his country. It meant fighting invaders. Everyone was willing to stand up for that.

He didn't see Duffy till Duffy grabbed his elbow. "I've got to talk to you," he said.

Gavin looked around. The .45 weighed heavily in the attaché case. He didn't want to talk to anyone—not with a hit only hours away.

But he didn't want to arouse Duffy's suspicions either. Duffy was close to the deal on some level, that much Gavin knew for sure.

"OK," Gavin said. He led Duffy to a quiet corner of the lobby on the far side from the house phones. "What is it?"

Duffy thought for a moment and then said, "I know you're a spook. I don't know who you are, or why you're here. But I bet it's got something to do with de Leon."

Duffy paused, and Gavin said nothing.

"Look," Duffy said. "I'm not here officially." He chuckled. "In fact, I might not be *anywhere* officially in a few days. I could be out on my ear as soon as I get back to Washington." Duffy considered the possibility for a few seconds, made up his mind about something, then continued. "I'm going to level with you. De Leon was working for me—a highly sensitive, highly classified mission."

"Sounds like he blew it."

Duffy looked angry. "I don't know what happened. All I know is that events turned crazy as soon as CIA stepped into the picture."

Gavin didn't want to hear any more of it. "Look," he said to Duffy. "I don't know

what you're talking about." He turned and
walked to the bank of elevators. He could
feel Duffy's gaze on his back. Gavin wanted
to get it over with, get the hell out of
Bahia as soon as possible. For Christ's
sakes, there were guys walking up to him
in hotel lobbies discussing hits! What kind
of upside-down deal was this?

Once in his room, Gavin undressed and
stretched out on the bed. It was eight
o'clock. He lighted a cigarette, inhaled
deeply, watching the ship's lights holding
steady in the windless heat.

Gavin smiled. He thought of the popular image people had of how the CIA and
other supersecret organizations work. All
space-age technology and mysterious methods of killing, all carried out in precise
digital synchronization.

In fact, it was lonely men like Gavin
loading .45's and blowing away other
lonely men who were on the other team.
Most Terminators liked to reduce the odds
by taking out their opposition numbers
while they were eating meals or getting
their rocks off atop hookers. Really tech-
nological guys would wire a car's ignition
to a few pounds of plastique and take out
half the neighborhood along with their
victim. It didn't matter. All that mattered
was that the right guy got killed too.

Gavin stubbed out the cigarette. He
thought of Duffy. The fat man had never

been in a more dangerous position. Duffy was lucky he was still alive. There were other Terminators who would have dumped Duffy out for what he said. When you're going to kill a man, you don't want to talk about it. And if someone starts talking to you about it, someone who shouldn't be talking, then that someone eats it too.

Maybe in other times, Gavin would have killed Duffy. He would have lured him outside, taken him for a walk, squeezed him until he talked—or didn't talk—and then eased him into the afterlife. But that wasn't going to happen now because Gavin didn't care anymore. It was just one more hit. Then he was out.

At 10:15 Gavin showered quickly, dressed in dark clothing, and tucked the .45 back into the attaché case. It would be nice to wear the weapon, but it was so hot that a man wearing a jacket would have stood out, and the gun was just too damned heavy to be tucked into a waistband.

At 10:30 he set off for National Security headquarters. He was outside the main entrance at 10:45, standing in the shadows, the attaché case gripped tightly.

The street in front of National Security was even busier then he remembered it from earlier in the evening. Traffic was dense. Pedestrians, mindless of the automobiles, crossed the street whenever they felt like it. Brakes squealed. Angry voices shouted curses. The scene was made to order for the kind of deal Gavin was in.

At 11:05 de Leon stepped onto the sidewalk, glanced both ways, and headed for the waterfront.

Gavin noted the sidearm.

Gavin fell in behind him, keeping his distance. It was impossible for de Leon to pick him out of the crowd and Gavin knew it. When de Leon entered a restaurant Gavin did too. De Leon ordered a meal, then lighted a cigarette. He kept glancing around. Finally his gaze settled on Gavin.

Gavin returned the look.

De Leon was no fool. He knew damned well that he was someone's target as soon as he was released. He wanted to get it over with as soon as possible.

De Leon stood up before his meal arrived and walked out of the restaurant. Gavin was behind him all the way. He followed the uniformed officer another four blocks, then saw de Leon duck into an alley.

It was as good a place as any.

Gavin came in low. He made it across the alley's entrance and behind a pallet of crates as the first shot rang out. He heard it blow into the wall to the right of him. He glanced out, saw de Leon break from cover and head up the alley.

Gavin stepped out quickly. He gripped the .45 in both hands and drew down steadily. He fired once. Gavin saw de Leon go forward on his face and lie still.

Gavin could hear screams and angry voices all around him. The gunfire had startled enough people to block both exits of the alley—Gavin had to move fast. He ran to the sprawled figure and saw that his round had taken de Leon in the back of the head.

That was that.

Gavin kept moving, tossing the .45 down as he ran. There were three figures at the alley's exit. Gavin barreled through them, kept running, and turned the corner.

Gavin joined the throng of pedestrians headed towards the waterfront. He slowed to a walk, blending with the crowd. Merchant seamen on shore for a good time gave the crowd just the look that Gavin needed. Young men dressed casually, blondes, redheads, a mix of types and nationalities allowed Gavin to pass unnoticed in their midst.

Finally, thirty minutes later, he walked through the lobby of La Florida and took the elevator to his floor. As he walked down the hall to his room, he felt exhausted, drained, and relieved that it was finally all over.

Downstairs in the lobby, Duffy stood by the house phones, puffing a cigarette. He had seen Gavin enter. It was clear that Gavin was on some sort of automatic pilot.

His face had appeared stony, his expression fixed. Duffy wondered what the hell had happened. He checked his watch, saw that it was almost midnight.

What had Gavin been up to?

He tossed the cigarette to the floor and stepped on the ember just as Colonel Rojas, accompanied by ten soldiers, entered the lobby.

The soldiers were carrying M-14's. They seemed totally out of place amidst the newsmen and communications crews still loitering in the lobby, anxious to get into the bar. Duffy watched as Rojas positioned men at the stairways leading down from the upper floors. As Rojas waited for the elevator, Duffy suddenly knew what he had to do. He picked up the house phone and asked the switchboard for Gavin's room.

Gavin sat on the edge of his bed as he finished his second shot of Jack Daniels. He felt at peace. A part of his life had ended. He could finally put down the guns that had been with him forever.

The phone rang.

For a moment Gavin stared at it. Then he picked it up.

"Gavin?" It was Duffy.

"What is it?"

"Look, Gavin. I don't know what's going on tonight, but if I were you, I'd pack up and get down to my room on the double. Rojas is on his way upstairs with about five soldiers. They don't look like they're inviting you a party."

"How the hell do you know they're after me?"

Duffy laughed. "I don't. Why don't you sit there and find out? Or why the hell don't you just get down to Room 312 and have a drink?"

The line went dead.

Duffy was right. This was no time to try to figure things out. Gavin left his room, went down four flights of stairs, and came out on the third floor. Duffy was waiting for him down the hall, out of breath. "Had to take the stairs," he told Gavin.

Duffy unlocked the door. They both entered the room. Duffy flicked on the light and sat on the bed. "Don't bother telling me that you don't know what's going on," Duffy said. "I don't want to hear it. I'm going back downstairs to see if I can find out what Rojas wants you for."

With a grunt he pushed himself to his feet and walked to the door. "I don't know why I'm bothering," he said to Gavin. "I have a feeling that I'm not going to like what I hear."

He left.

nine _____

Colonel Rojas had a problem on his hands.

The idea had been simplicity itself. As soon as de Leon was killed, Gavin would be arrested and charged with the crime: A *loco* American who decided to take justice into his own hands and kill the murderous de Leon to avenge the deaths of the innocent missionaries. Then, in a cell, remorseful for his act, Gavin hangs himself.

But where was Gavin? He should have been in his room. The desk clerk said that Gavin had entered the hotel. Did he not go to his room?

What Colonel Rojas had not counted on was the crowd. Who was to think that events in Costa Bella had generated so much attention that the hotel's lobby would be so crowded? He could not very well conduct a room by room search when many of the rooms were occupied by members of the international press. There would be too many questions to answer. "How was Gavin identified so quickly after the shooting of de Leon?" "How was it established that he was staying at La Florida?"

Rojas's head ached with the implications.

"Basta!" He called off his men and left the hotel. There was no way out of the country for Gavin. He had no one to turn to for help. Layton, the American CIA resident, was filled with formaldehyde inside a wood box at the airport awaiting a flight home.

No. Gavin had little to do now. He could hide for a while, but sooner or later he would surface. When he did it would be over.

In the meantime, Colonel Rojas would release the information that de Leon had been murdered by an insane American and he would wait him out.

It wasn't so bad, Rojas thought. In a way, it actually looked better this way. A bit of delay between the crime and the capture—a certain amount of suspense. It satisfied his sense of the dramatic.

Duffy belched.

Gavin was groggy with lack of sleep and whiskey. It had been a long night. "And that's it," Duffy said. "De Leon was doing the job for me. It blew up in our faces."

Gavin leaned back and fixed his gaze on a crack in the ceiling plaster. "So what you're telling me," he said to Duffy," is that I killed an innocent man. Worse—I killed a man working for us."

"That's about it," Duffy said.

"You don't believe that de Leon was involved in the murder of the four missionaries?"

Gavin was looking for a way out, an exit from the sudden weight of awful guilt. Duffy shrugged. "He was involved," Duffy said. "Against his will, probably. He wasn't that kind of guy."

Gavin nodded. It was what he always dreaded. The sure knowledge that he had hit a good guy. With the others, there had never been any doubts. But the de Leon assignment had been wrong from the beginning.

And it was still going on.

Her name was Maria Angela Garcia y Olguin. She was the daughter of the minister of the interior. She was a beautiful brunette, not yet twenty years old, and Colonel Rojas was proud to number her among his mistresses.

He had taken her roughly this time. She had squirmed with discomfort, which only added to his pleasure. She was standing, leaning forward across his desk, as he entered her from behind.

Rojas liked to make love in his office, aware that outside the door his many visitors were seated, awaiting their turns. He knew that it added to Maria's humiliation, but that was all right too.

Her father's position depended on the military's endorsement of him, and to a large degree that depended on Rojas.

When he finished he zipped up his pants, took his seat behind the desk, and watched Maria as she dressed. She pulled a white dress over her head, then ran her hands through her long, thick hair.

"It is always a pleasure with you," he said.

She smiled. "You are a fantastic lover," she said in her low, warm voice. "But what a shame that you must leave. When will you be back?"

He shrugged. "It is a patrol in the Oriente, and that sometimes takes longer than one assumes," Rojas said. "But don't worry—I shall call as soon as I return."

Maria came to him. She kissed him warmly on the lips. "Until then," she said softly.

Rojas buzzed his secretary as soon as Maria had left. "Who is next?" he asked.

"Señor Duffy," said the gruff voice of his secretary, a sergeant who provided an extra touch of security.

"Ah. Duffy. Send him in."

Duffy was grinning when he walked in. Rojas didn't like it. "Good day, Señor Duffy," he said. "What can I do for you today?"

Duffy sat down without being asked. The heat of Bahia had left him permanently red faced. "Not much," Duffy said. "Just wanted to ask a few questions. I'll be leaving today. I wanted to know how the search is going for the killer of de Leon."

"Ah. What a shame that whole matter is," Rojas said, shaking his head. "I am sad to say that I have nothing to report. Of course we have put out descriptions of Señor Gavin, and when we apprehend him I can assure you that he will receive a speedy, just trial."

"But so far . . ."

"But so far, we have not found him. That is curious, of course. We have devoted many men and many hours to the search. But as you well know, the city of Bahia is caught in the middle of a civil war. The population has other things on its mind. There is money being made, Señor Duffy. People do not have the time or the inclination to search for an obscure American who has murdered a monster."

"I can see that."

"I shall be leaving on a patrol to the Oriente," Rojas said carelessly. "But when I return I shall be glad to forward to your office any information we have come across."

"I guess that'll have to do," Duffy said. "Sure wish I could have talked to de Leon before he was released."

"Who was to know that a killer was on

his trail? But justice will be done—you have my assurance of that," Rojas concluded.

Duffy took a cab back to the hotel. It was but a fifteen minute walk, but Duffy didn't want to exert himself at all in the intense heat. He had not been feeling well. He was positive that it was nothing but the change of climate. Still, the night before he had had heart palpitations, and Gavin had forced him to drink about a third of a bottle of bourbon, telling him that it was a proven remedy.

It had calmed the heart palpitations, but Duffy still wasn't sure it was the thing to do.

Gavin was waiting for him in the room. He looked strange with his black hair— Duffy had dyed it for him the day before with supplies purchased at the pharmacy down the street.

"What did he say?" Gavin asked immediately.

"Not much. The search is still on. But it's been two days, and they really don't know what to do. Here's what I learned: Rojas is going off on patrol tomorrow— might be a good idea if you tagged along."

"Are you nuts?"

"Look, I'm checking out today. Where the hell are you going to go? You're going to have to get out of this country by crossing the border on foot. They'll be waiting for you at all the official crossings."

"I guess I'll join the Costa Bellan Army tonight then, and shove off in the morning with Rojas."

Duffy smiled. "I've got a thousand dollars I can let you have. Do what you can with it. All I know is that Rojas is off to Oriente Province—see what happens on the way. It's the route you'll have to take out anyway. You've got nothing to lose."

Gavin smiled. "Nothing to lose. I like the sound of that. Here I am, with the entire country searching for me, with the army on the alert to blow me to dogmeatland as soon as they see me, and you say I've got nothing to lose."

Gavin lighted a cigarette. He walked to the window. The view from the third floor was not as good as that from the seventh, but the ships at the waterfront still beckoned. "Isn't there any way I can slip aboard one of those babies?"

"Beats me," Duffy said. "I'm just a tired old lawyer from the Justice Department who hates to see a fellow American in the shitcan. Hell, I don't know why I got mixed up in this anyway. De Leon was my man, and you killed him."

"Yeah."

"Here's the money." Duffy handed Gavin an envelope stuffed with twenties. "When you get out, get in touch with me."

Gavin smiled. "Not *if* you get out. *When* you get out." He tucked away the money and shook Duffy's hand. "Maybe I'll see you," he said. "If I don't—well, it's almost been a pleasure."

The sun was bright and warm at the Santa Monica Airport. Dr. Willard Lee completed his walk-around inspection of the brand new Cessna Stationair 8. Modified with an extra set of long-range fuel tanks, it still provided 300 pounds in baggage allowance. Powered by a Teledyne Continental IO-520-F fuel-injection engine, the Cessna was more than adequate for what Dr. Lee had to do.

It was already loaded with medical supplies. He shook hands with the ground crew and climbed aboard. He was glad that he'd decided to leave without the usual hoopla generated by the local television news crews. He'd had enough of that.

Simple. Straight down to Costa Bella, then straight back. The last load.

He wondered if Barnes would let him walk away cleanly. Or whether he'd have to explain to Barnes that if anything happened to him, his attorney would have certain documents that would take Barnes over the side to.

He lifted off easily, climbing to 12,000 feet as he flew south.

ten _____

"Five hundred dollars?"

The young Costa Bellan nodded vigor-
ously, a grin across his face. *Quinientos
dólares*—five hoondred," he said in English.

Gavin looked at the bike. It was a ten-
year-old BSA 250. It sounded like the trans
was about to become history. But he needed
transportation and this was as good as it
was going to get.

"Here," Gavin said, counting out twenty-
five twenty dollar bills. The young man
nodded, counting along with Gavin. Finally
he said, *"Buena suerte."*

"Thanks," Gavin answered. "I'm going
to need it."

He climbed on and cranked the machine
to life. It roared, its muffler long gone. He
eased out into traffic and threaded his way
towards the waterfront. He felt safer there,
comfortable among the many foreigners
clogging the bars and restaurants on the
Malecon.

During daylight hours it was too dangerous to be seen alone—even though Duffy's dye job had turned his hair flat black. Gavin knew that such minor alterations couldn't be counted on.

Gavin pulled up in front of a sidewalk cafe, kicked down the stand on the bike, and took a table not five feet away from his machine. That would be all he needed right now, having the bike burned off the street while he dumped a few beers.

He ordered a dark beer and ceviche, a cocktail of raw fish steeped in lime juice. The juice cooked the fish, Gavin knew, and the taste—spicy as hell—was perfect.

As he ate, Gavin thought about his predicament. It had only been four days since he left High Card, Colorado, on what was supposed to have been his last mission. Now, his entire world was upside down. He still couldn't see a way out.

He was unarmed, and that made him feel highly vulnerable. He had no official support—what assassin does? For all he knew, Washington had washed their hands of him. In fact, he wouldn't be surprised to learn that that prick, Barnes, had gone along with the Costa Bellan Government and let them hang up his picture in the post office.

Truly fucked is what it was.

"I don't give a damn, Al. It's like passing up easy money!"

The two Americans at the next table were

middle-aged, tan, and looked right at home. They weren't tourists—Gavin was beginning to wonder if there were any pure and simple tourists in Bahia.

They were newsmen, used to covering international hot spots.

"Look, we'll have everything but the stills. And for chrissakes, I'll buy a camera and take the damned pictures myself!"

The other man was shaking his head. "No. We need a pro on this one. People start shooting, I can just see you taking pictures! Who're you kidding? You'll be under the truck with me!"

Gavin wanted to wait until dusk, then take the road leading west and get out of Bahia before dark. It was the kind of war he knew well. Not a lot of night fighting—mainly daylight skirmishes with both sides respecting an unofficial evening curfew.

Out in the countryside after dark would be safer for Gavin than in Bahia. He feared the rebels less than the Costa Bellan armed forces. Besides, if Rojas left on patrol tomorrow, that would be the road he'd take.

Gavin could tag along.

"Otra cerveza?" Gavin looked up and smiled. She was by far the loveliest thing he'd seen in quite a while. Long black hair reached midway down her back, framing a small-featured face with bright brown eyes and luscious red lips. She was small, perhaps five feet two inches, and built like

a ballerina, tightly muscled, and exciting because of it.

"Si," Gavin replied, and she emptied the bottle into his glass and set off for a fresh one. He sipped slowly, enjoying the bit of freedom.

On the curb three young boys passed an American cigarette from hand to hand. Bahia was poor, even though the city was bustling with commercial activity. On the hills that bordered the city, squatters had thrown up lean-tos and mud huts, lured to the capital by tales of quick and easy money. But there was no quick and easy money in a place like Bahia, Gavin thought. Only the same old wartime hustles that he remembered from Saigon.

She brought another beer and put it down in front of him, and this time Gavin noticed a new look in her eyes: fear. He smiled at her, keeping it casual, and when she walked away from the table he let his gaze follow her, a smile of appreciation on his face. He could see them out of the corner of his eye—two of them, young recruits from the way they held themselves.

They were armed with assault rifles and they looked edgy enough to use them.

Gavin finished his beer, tossed a twenty peso bill on the table, and stepped over the low fence separating the tables from the sidewalk. He didn't even glance at the two soldiers.

He kicked the bike to life, put on a pair of sunglasses, and wheeled out into traffic.

Duffy had on his new blue suit and a freshly laundered shirt. He had been waiting outside the Oval Office for forty-five minutes, and Jed Anderson was trying to make conversation.

"We don't get many Justice people up here. Maybe the attorney general. That's about it."

"I can understand that."

"You met a week ago with the President. Hope things worked out."

"Perfectly," Duffy said with a smile. His mouth was dry and he was wondering how Gavin was doing. There had been no word out of Costa Bella.

The door to the Oval Office opened and the President's chief of staff, Ed Nelson, stepped out. He smiled when he saw Duffy and beckoned him to come in.

The President was on the phone, his feet on the desk. It was a political call—a new Chicago alderman was phoning in his thanks for the President's support.

The President waved Duffy to a chair and then took about thirty seconds to get off the phone. "Well, Duffy," he said. "It looks like we have a problem."

"We do," Duffy said. "And I don't really know what to do about it."

"Welcome home," the President said with a grin. "First off, I'd like to tell you that I don't like circumstances—and this entire de Leon situation is not to my liking at all."

Duffy was stunned. Was there hope? "Mr. President," Duffy said, "I couldn't agree more."

"Now I know that you advised against bringing CIA into this," the President continued. "And I must say that, in hindsight, perhaps bringing them in was a mistake. I say *perhaps*. There is also a probable likelihood that Mr. de Leon was exactly the brute he appeared to be."

"I don't think so. In any case, de Leon's situation is academic. I have no other agent in place."

"I see." The President thought for a moment and then said, "Suppose I delay this for another week. I should be able to buy that much time. Is there anything you can do for me on such short notice?"

Duffy agonized. He didn't want to tell the President that he had harbored de Leon's killer—it would have made a farce of the entire event. He liked Gavin—but what if the man was a pathological type, and Duffy hadn't been able to see through him?

"Mr. President, I might have another

option open—but I think you'll understand that perhaps I should play this one a bit closer to the vest. That way there will be no doubt, and no circumstances, if and when it develops."

The sudden anger in the President's face startled Duffy, and he swallowed hard before the President answered. "I won't take that the wrong way," he said. "I won't think that you're saying that this isn't a secure office. I don't know exactly how I will take it—we can get to that later."

"Thank you, Mr. President."

"A week, Duffy. That's it. And I might as well tell you right now that I'm leaning toward sending in as much materiel as I can get away with. Equipment, advisors, the whole shot. We can't afford another Nicaragua, or another El Salvador. Castro's done nothing but instigate trouble for over twenty years, and I feel—damnit, and I think I'm right—that Costa Bella's as good a place to stop him as any if he's mixed up there."

"Yes sir."

"A week, Duffy. And good luck."

A half hour later Duffy was at his desk in the Justice Department, trying to figure out how to get word to Gavin. If Gavin was what he said—and Duffy believed him— there was no reason that Gavin couldn' do the job.

Unless he got killed, of course.

*   *   *

Gavin awoke at first light.

The temperature was around eighty degrees, and it felt cool, considering what was coming. He drank water from his canteen and ate two bread rolls. The highway down which Rojas's column would be moving was quiet.

Gavin was bone tired. Not so much from the night under the stars, or any other physical reason. He had spent fifteen years killing people, and it was supposed to be all over.

Gavin didn't want it anymore. He wanted the peace and the security of High Card, and he wanted the pleasure and the companionship of Kendall.

He took another drink from the canteen, screwed down the top, and stashed it on the bike. There were crawling bugs, most of which bit, and in a half hour he was covered with dozens of bites, itchy and burning.

Then he saw the column coming down the highway.

Gavin counted two jeeps, four troop transports, and four supply trucks. They moved by at a good pace. Gavin gave them fifteen minutes, then cranked up the bike and fell in behind them.

It was so dry that the dust from the highway's shoulders raised up and gave Gavin the column's position as he tagged along.

When the dust stopped, Gavin stopped.

Gavin ditched the bike. He made his way on foot toward the noise ahead. He was unarmed, in hostile territory. All normal exits were closed to him: airports, bus or train stations, highway border crossings.

He knew that through some agency snafu he had killed a man who shouldn't have been killed.

Ahead, the Costa Bellan military gave a demonstration of what not to do, making enough noise and raising enough dust to attract the most unobservant enemy. They were clearly unconcerned with that possibility.

The sounds of automatic-rifle fire stopped Gavin in his tracks. Maybe Rojas and his column hit an ambush, rebel guerrillas giving them a lesson in Military Basic 101.

Gavin was on his belly. The firefight aroma wafted to him as he lay still. Ahead, he now heard voices. The shooting was over.

He heard Rojas's voice.

Gavin crawled to a small rise, moving easily through the scrub. Finally he saw the village.

It was small and primitive, perhaps twenty mud-and-thatch buildings. Rojas stood in the midst of perhaps thirty bodies, slick with blood. Pink puckered flesh and white bone showed where the automatic fire had effected amputations.

Rojas yelled out an order in Spanish. Gavin watched as the four men near one of the transports started unloading rifles. The rifles were distributed among the corpses.

Rojas checked out the disposition of the weapons, moving them under the arms of a few of the corpses. Then he called for the film crew, and they began shooting 16mm motion pictures of the massacre.

Of course, Rojas would announce that the bodies were those of rebel forces, killed during a firefight. Who was going to say otherwise?

The harsh sun had turned Gavin's face sore to the touch, but there was no way to seek shade. He crouched, quiet, and watched.

Every now and then Rojas wandered over to one of the transports and checked with the men guarding it. Gavin noticed that only one transport truck was guarded, the others were deserted.

What the hell was in that truck?

Gavin heard the sound of crinkling brush to his right. He flattened slowly, then parted the grass in front of him. He saw a lone soldier from Rojas's group moving slowly toward him.

The soldier, a kid of nineteen or so, hadn't seen him yet. Gavin eased back, down the rise, then turned and crawled quickly towards the heavier scrub.

The soldier kept coming.

Gavin could hear his footfalls as he plodded through the brush. Gavin's throat was dry and tickley. He was breathing through his nose to forestall a cough.

He heard the drone of a small plane. He checked the sky and saw nothing.

The footsteps grew closer.

Gavin made his move while the young soldier's back was to him. He locked a forearm around his neck, dragged him quickly and silently to the ground. Gavin compressed hard and collapsed the soldier's throat.

Gavin held him until he stopped kicking.

He stripped off the AK-47 and as many clips as he could manage. He crawled back to the rise and was suddenly conscious once again of the airplane's droning sound.

It was much louder now.

Gavin rolled over onto his back just in time to witness the Cessna pass over him at perhaps two hundred feet, wagging his wings, telling everyone where Gavin was.

He heard Rojas bark commands. He heard the answering shouts of the squad leaders as they came forward towards Gavin.

He poked his head above the rise and drew immediate fire. They were coming straight on. This time Gavin slid the assault rifle out first. He fired a forty-five degree burst, then turned tail for the deeper scrub cover.

He crashed headfirst into the tall grass and crawled towards the wooded area ahead. There was a plain to cross, a hundred yards of fairly open territory.

Gavin knew he'd never get across it alive.

He hit the edge of the tall grass and scanned the open field. A hundred yards to the woods. He heard a noise to his left, then saw a troop transport careen into the open field, blocking his exit. Troops jumped out, fanned, and began moving towards the tall grass.

Behind him Gavin heard the other troops making their way slowly towards him through the grass. Short bursts of automatic fire told him that they weren't asking any questions. Anything that moved was something to shoot at.

What bullshit this is, thought Gavin.

He could easily hear their voices now. He eased up into a prone position and fired a burst shin-high through the grass. The screams of those he hit were less impressive than the hail of returned fire.

It seemed like too much fire to come from the number of troops that Gavin had seen. Or was it his own death fear that was augmenting the sounds?

There were shouts behind him, from the open plain. What the hell was going on? The fire was directed over his head, back into the woods.

The troops were being fired on by guerrillas hidden in the woods!

Gavin came up in a crouch and headed
back toward the village. Most of the troops
had passed him by in their rush to meet
their death in the withering fire pouring
from the woods.

Ahead Gavin saw that the Cessna had
landed. Rojas and two soldiers were loading canvas bags into the hold. Gavin fired
a burst at three soldiers heading his way.
That was when Rojas spotted him.

There was dirt erupting in a zigzag line
toward him, so Gavin jumped to his left
and rolled. Then he was on his feet again,
a fresh clip fed into the AK-47, pouring
fire toward the plane.

He saw Rojas jump in and the Cessna
taxi away. He ran forward, blowing away
two soldiers who came out from behind a
transport truck.

The Cessna lifted easily into the blue
sky, barely easing out of range.

The firefight had stopped. As Gavin
turned around he saw the band of guerrillas
slowly drifting out of the woods, inspecting
the soldiers' bodies as they came forward.

Two of the guerrillas had their automatic
weapons leveled on Gavin's chest. He knew
that there was no way out of this one.

He tossed the AK-47 into the vegetation
and put his hands atop his head.

eleven _____

The insects were swarming, eager for a carcass picnic. As Gavin watched the armed guerrillas slowly approaching him, he was surprised to see that many of them seemed to be little more than children.

There were a few hard-eyed men, and they were in charge. But the bulk of the fighting force was made up of fifteen-year-old boys barely able to handle their weapons.

And there was a woman.

She was absolutely out of place. Gavin had seen enough female troops to know that the field hardened a woman faster than it did a man. But she looked like she could put down her rifle and sit down for a cocktail without even changing clothes. She was brunette, fresh faced, red lipped, with a lush young body that made Gavin regret his possible impending death even more.

She was in charge. She called off the gunmen and walked up to Gavin. "You are American?" she asked. She ran her tongue over her lower lip, glossing it.

"Yes," Gavin said.

"You are Gavin," she said, her eyes widening in recognition.

"I am," he answered.

Then she smiled. "You are quite well known," she said. "Rojas saw to it before he left Bahia. You are wanted for the murder of that animal, de Leon."

"I am," Gavin answered. His hands were still clasped atop his head. He'd wait till she said to put them down.

"And here you are, alone, encircled by Rojas and his men. Why are you not seeking your freedom? How is it that you are still in Costa Bella?"

"There was no easy way out. If there had been, I'd have taken it."

She studied him silently for a moment. "I should have you killed, of course."

"Of course? Why of course?"

"Because the United States plans to aid men like Rojas. Because my men will wonder why an American should receive special treatment."

Gavin glanced at the hard male eyes surrounding him. To expect mercy from those eyes would be to expect sweet milk from rocks.

"But then they do not know about you, Señor Gavin. They have been in the field, out of touch."

"Who are you?"

"My name is unimportant. I had obtained

knowledge that Rojas would be on this road. We observed you all the while you were tracking him. We prepared the ambush as we did because we had planned to use you to bait the trap. You did it for us."

"My pleasure."

"Of course, if the airplane had not flown over . . ."

"Did you get the markings?" Gavin had not. All he remembered was a red cross— was it a medical plane?

"We will talk later," the dark-haired woman said. She turned and barked a few commands, and moments later Gavin's hands were bound behind his back.

They set off on foot toward the south.

Barnes received word of the ambush that destroyed Rojas's column before that information was forwarded to Washington by conventional means.

Barnes sat slumped at his desk. It had not been a good day. The White House was more than a little upset with the way the de Leon matter had turned out. That reaction was to be expected. But when Lee called on an open line—an open line!—and told Barnes what had happened, that was when Barnes troubles began.

First of all, the open line. Dr. Willard Lee certainly knew better than to contact Barnes in such a manner. There was no telling who was listening in.

But even supposing that no one was listening, Barnes was still not home free. Lee carefully explained how the pick-up had turned around on them. How Gavin apparently had been tracking Rojas, how he had started a firefight, how Rojas had had to jump aboard with Dr. Lee in order to save his miserable life.

There was a touch of good news: rebels had been in the area and had opened fire on the government forces during the firefight with Gavin. Supposedly, the rebels had wasted little time in executing Gavin, if he wasn't already killed in the firefight.

Barnes was worried.

Rojas was with Dr. Willard Lee in California. That had taken some careful flying by Lee. He'd managed to put down, unload the cargo, and leave Rojas in the warehouse near Ventura along with the cargo.

Barnes had a drugged-out medico and a sadistic military monster on his hands. Lee sounded as if he were crumbling fast. He would have to be dealt with.

Like Gavin, Dr. Lee had just performed his last mission for Barnes and was looking for the pleasures of a well-funded retirement. Like Gavin, Lee would be terminated. The Agency never retired men like that. It simply killed them. Far more cost efficient, far more secure.

Rojas was another matter. It would be best to return him to Costa Bella to oversee the operation until Barnes could locate another means of transportation. Dr. Lee was useless—his drugs had made him too unreliable. His retirement was a certainty.

Barnes stood up, removed his trench coat from the coatrack by the door, and left the office. As he walked down the now-empty hall in the CIA complex in Langley, Virginia, he wondered if it was going to work out.

So many years in the planning. And with the money just now starting to roll in. The last flight should be worth a half million at least, Barnes thought.

He was building up a little nest egg. He didn't want anything to botch the deal.

As he showed his ID to the guard stationed at the door to Parking Lot E, Barnes shivered, thinking of Gavin.

"Pretty damned cold outside," he said to Barnes, who glanced at the handsome young man. The guard was a lean, tough-looking blond with hard eyes and a cruel mouth.

Barnes felt the sudden surge of sexual energy. He would have loved to take this young man home with him.

But that would have been considered an unpardonable lapse in security.

The next morning Duffy stumbled to work with a hangover that, even by his standards, was one for the record books. He slumped behind his desk to wait till he'd had three cups of coffee before making a move.

The folder on his desk had attracted his eyes as soon as he'd walked into the office. When he finally opened it he smiled.

It was a report from Costa Bella, sent over to Duffy from the White House. Colonel Rojas had apparently been ambushed, the report said, after Rojas carried out an execution in the small village of Punta Alta.

One of the villagers had survived the massacre by feigning death. He had witnessed the landing of a medical aircraft, an attack by a single crazed *americano*, and the intervention of the rebels.

The Costa Bellan Government discounted the peasant's tale of outright murder on the part of Rojas, as well as the rest of his story. It was passed along in the form of raw intelligence, and would probably find few believers in official Washington.

But Duffy was one of them.

So Gavin was still alive, and raising hell. Duffy grinned. Gavin was obviously a vengeful man behind that indifferent, cool exterior. Being set up and double-crossed had made Gavin angry. Very angry. According to the report, seventy-five government troops were killed in the firefight.

That was the heaviest loss ever suffered in a single operation by the armed forces of Costa Bella.

Duffy still didn't have the slightest idea of how to get in touch with Gavin, but that was all right. The White House had seen this report. Added to all the other things they now knew, Duffy felt that he had bought himself a bit more time.

He wondered is Gavin was still alive.

Inside the mud hut the temperature was cooler than the furnace-like heat outdoors. Gavin was lying on his back, the hard-packed earth cool against his skin.

The hut was perhaps ten feet by ten feet— a large closet. The one doorway was obscured by an overhang to keep out the sun.

Outside, a sentry paced in front of the hut.

Gavin shook his last cigarette from the pack, crushed the box, and then lighted the Marlboro. He hadn't talked to anyone since the rebels had brought him in. He didn't know where he was.

He knew there was a good chance they would make him kneel down in front of an open pit while they expanded his consciousness permanently with a bullet in the back of the head. He was, after all, an *americano*. All the *americanos* had ever done was arm and support the brutes who ran the country.

It was senseless trying to explain that

Americans didn't support tyrannies. Our government did, and that was enough.

Gavin put his mind off the subject of his own survival. It was a depressing situation. He would have to wait for a break, or take whatever opportunity presented itself.

He thought about the medical plane that had given away his position to Rojas.

It didn't make any sense. The markings appeared to be American, and the plane wasn't on any mission of mercy. It was there to pick up whatever Rojas and his troops had so carefully guarded all the way to the village.

Rojas had been an unexpected passenger. Gavin smiled as he thought of the discomfort Rojas must be causing whoever was in the command position on that operation. Subhumans like Rojas didn't travel well. In another country, stripped of his life-and-death powers, a man like Rojas could crumble quickly and incur no end of problems.

They would have to keep him out of the way until they figured out what to do.

So Rojas was probably holed up somewhere, swearing in two languages, anxious and eager to get back to his homeland to open a few bellies in celebration of his repatriation.

Voices outside the hut made Gavin sit up. He recognized the brunette's voice. She seemed to be instructing the sentry.

Was this it? Was the sentry going to order Gavin outside for a last look at reality?

The sentry came in with her, standing in the doorway, his assault rifle leveled at Gavin. She sat down across from Gavin and said, "We will be leaving soon."

"Where to?" he asked.

"To Bahia. It has been decided that you shall live."

"I feel like I should thank someone."

She grinned. "Thank me. You see, I had special information. I know that you had been to see Rojas in Bahia. I told the others that you were clearly a member of some underground organization in the United States, a group that favored our cause. Such groups exist, I know."

"Yes," Gavin said.

"I explained that it was in our own interests to return you to the United States so that you might inform others of the true conditions here."

"Full-page ads. That'll do the trick."

"We must make the American Government understand that it has nothing to fear from people who want to govern themselves and enjoy the same freedoms that are described in your Bill of Rights."

"I couldn't agree more." Gavin was anxious to get going. They could politic until they all turned to stone and it wouldn't change a damned thing. Besides, Gavin had no intention of devoting his life to someone else's fight. He had enough on his own plate.

"We will take you to Bahia," she said. "Then we shall arrange for transportation to the United States."

"I can't just walk into the country," he said. "They'll probably be waiting for me. I've got get in without being noticed."

She grinned. "That is not difficult," she said. "We shall move you first to Nicaragua, and from there to Cuba. From Cuba it is but a short ride to Florida."

"That's right," Gavin said.

She frowned. "Your journey would have been much simpler," she said, "if Ivanovich had not been assassinated. He handled many people for us. The Russians provide many services to our cause. They have shown by their deeds that they are friendly to the people."

Gavin stood up. "Is that guy going to keep that rifle pointed at me all the time?" he asked.

She waved off the sentry. "You are free," she said.

"I don't even know your name," Gavin said.

She smiled. "Maria Angela Garcia y Olguin," she said. "My father is a member of the government. I am the mistress of Rojas."

Gavin smiled.

"I must do it in order to steal whatever information I can," she said haughtily. "If I had not been submitting to him, so that I learned where he was going, you would be dead now."

"You're going to think I'm pretty dumb," Gavin said, glancing at the rebel holding the rifle. "But why are you telling me all this?"

She smiled. "I have to," she said.

"Why?"

"It was a command decision. They said that if I was going to vouch for you, then I had to demonstrate my faith." She shrugged. "With what I have told you, my life is worth nothing if you tell the authorities in Bahia."

"How are they going to know what you told me? You could have lied."

She pointed to the rebel. "Jorge understands English perfectly," Maria Angela said.

Jorge grinned suddenly. "She speaks the truth," he said.

Gavin said, "When do we leave?"

"Now," Maria Angela answered.

twelve

A thunderstorm had turned the unpaved streets of Bahia to canals of mud. The four-wheel-drive jeep crept slowly down the back street. The driver, a silent, muscular man, eased over to the curb and Maria Angela stepped out. "This way," she said to Gavin, who followed her.

The streets were brightly lit by newly installed floodlights. On the corners, armed patrols stood, smoking, keeping the civilians under surveillance.

Maria Angela cut through an alley and then through the grounds of a large house painted white with a red tile roof. The grounds were well kept. The woodwork of the house was in excellent shape.

She went in through the back door with Gavin close behind.

"Very nice," Gavin said.

"It is my father's home," she said. "For now we are alone."

They were in a large foyer area, tiles underfoot, white walls on all sides. To the left was a living room, rectangular in shape, furnished in leather and wood. The interior of the house was cool, an effect of the thick walls and high ceilings.

Maria Angela led Gavin upstairs. She showed him to a small, neat bedroom and said, "Rest. I will call you when it is time to move." She reached into her pack and withdrew a Walther P-38 pistol. Maria Theresa glanced at Gavin and smiled. "This is for you," she said. She handed him the pistol, then dug out of her pack a total of twenty-four rounds for the weapon. Gavin checked it out. It was fully loaded, its magazine containing eight rounds.

Gavin felt much better with some sort of firepower. He knew that it wasn't much considering what the opposition was lugging around Bahia: automatic rifles of all types. Costa Bella had been buying arms from many different sources. That was reflected in the visible armament.

"Tonight we will move," Maria Angela said. She licked her lips, her face suddenly flushed and hot. Gavin glanced at the bed. When he looked up, Maria Angela was smiling. She slowly walked toward Gavin and encircled his waist with her arms. He leaned toward her, feeling his body answer hers.

Gavin led her to the bed.

*   *   *

Rojas was in a foul mood.

Dr. Willard Lee had not bothered to conceal his displeasure at having Rojas along for the ride back from Costa Bella. That, Rojas thought, was a serious mistake for the doctor to make. Rojas didn't like to be treated as an unwelcome guest. He would think of some way to make Dr. Willard Lee appreciate his error.

Rojas was sitting at a wood-top desk in the warehouse near Ojai, California, shivering in the cool night air. He had always been under the impression that southern California was a warm, green patch of earth, like Costa Bella. Rojas did not appreciate the browns and beiges of the California landscape. The chill night air was too much for his tropical blood.

The warehouse was down a dirt road near a stable that housed horses privately owned by successful individuals who lived in the city and therefore had to board their horses. The area in general—including the small village of Ojai—was well kept. It smelled strongly of money, and Rojas had an appreciation of that.

Outside, the blond man called Ted turned off the spigot and tossed the hose to the ground. He had been watering the grounds around the warehouse. He had told Rojas that he was allergic to the dust. He wanted to tamp it down.

He entered the warehouse. Rojas called

to him. Rojas watched the burly figure walk towards him. Ted carried a .45 in a covered holster. He wore Levi's, a t-shirt, and running shoes.

He, like his employer, Dr. Lee, did not seem to hold Rojas in the high regard that Rojas demanded of his associates. Rojas motioned for Ted to sit down. He poured the blond man a few ounces of the excellent Irish whiskey that Lee had left. "Tell me," Rojas said after he poured a drink for himself. "When will Dr. Lee return?"

Ted shrugged. He sipped the Bushmill's and considered Rojas. Ted didn't like the setup at all. The business was tough enough—and plenty dangerous—without Lee having to fuck it all up by bringing this clown back with him. Ted had seen it happen before. A good, smooth operation netting everyone a fortune. Then a Latin American shows up and right after that the whole deal takes a shit, and lots of people wind up shot dead.

Rojas looked like a killer. He was armed too. Ted liked that even less. It was one thing to nursemaid a warehouse stocked with five million dollars worth of heroin and cocaine. It was another thing to have to keep your eyes open for a snake like this.

"The only thing I know, see, is that Dr. Lee said he'd be back today. He never did tell me what time exactly. So you just relax, kick back, you know. He'll be here, don't worry."

Rojas nodded. "And the others? Where are they?"

Ted had two other men with him. "They're checking around the perimeter," Ted answered, thinking Rojas would like the military term. Ted wasn't sure what it meant.

Rojas caught the insolent intent behind Ted's words. He longed to put a round between the blond man's sheeplike eyes. But that would have to wait. Rojas was in the United States, far from Costa Bella. He had no papers, and could not afford to explain his transportation.

Ted finished his whiskey. He stood up. "See you later," he said. He turned and walked to the metal door. When Ted opened it the warehouse flooded with light. The door closed with an echoing clang and Rojas poured himself another whiskey.

By the time Barnes reached Georgetown it was seven-thirty and raining. He parked near the university and walked three blocks to the Cafe Donato. Under his arm he held a smooth leather portfolio.

Barnes was sweating.

He passed the cafe, circled the block, then backtracked to the small, exclusive cafe. Inside, sitting in a booth at the rear of the L-shaped room, was a heavy man in a dark blue suit, striped rep tie, and immaculate cordovans. He looked eminently respectable.

Barnes sat down across from him. "Make it quick," the heavy man said. At close range his face was coarse-featured, thick and lumpy. His impassive eyes stared through Barnes.

"It was an unfortunate error," Barnes said quickly. "It never should have happened."

"Yeah, yeah," the coarse-featured man said. "I've heard that before."

"But we have the situation well in hand now," Barnes continued.

The other man shifted in the booth. "Well in hand? You've got some madman from Costa Bella sitting in the California warehouse. You've got a pilot who's ready to flip out. And you've got a highly trained assassin somewhere wondering what the hell is going on."

"Let's take it step by step," Barnes said, falling back on his years of Agency training. "Rojas is not a problem. We'll have him out of the country shortly. Until then, the security at the warehouse is top flight."

"Oh boy," the other man said.

"Dr. Lee will be attended to very soon. I agree that he has become a dangerous liability. We both knew that sooner or later he would have to go. Now's the time."

"We'll handle it," the other man said.

"And as for Gavin—he's as good as dead."

Barnes opened the leather portfolio and extracted a large photo, eight inches by eleven. It was a blowup of Gavin's last official photograph, taken when he started with the Agency eight years before.

"So?"

"So Gavin should never walk out of Costa Bella," Barnes said. "But if he does, get him."

The other man's thick fingers held the print carefully by the edges. "You want me to put out a general contract on this guy, right?"

Barnes nodded. "Cover all points of entry. Also focus on Los Angeles. If he finds out anything, he'll probably head there."

The heavy man nodded, placing the photo face down on the table. "I hope for your sake this all works out," he said to Barnes.

Barnes worked up a smile. "It will," he said. "I've never failed yet."

When Gavin awoke, night had fallen and he could hear Maria Angela coming up the stairs.

She opened the bedroom door and said, "Come with me." He arose and tucked the P-38 into his waistband. He followed her down the stairs, yawning away the vestiges of sleep. He had needed the rest.

Downstairs, two glum-faced young men awaited them. She said something to them in Spanish. She turned to Gavin. "There is increased security because of the disappearance of Rojas," she said. "All of his associates are being arrested for questioning by the Security Police. They feel that he was betrayed." She smiled. "They will arrest me soon. I shall tell them nothing."

Gavin nodded. He had heard talk like that before, but he knew that everyone talked eventually. He hoped that she would make it easy on herself.

"Good luck," he said softly, kissing her on the cheek. She was warm and smooth to the touch. Gavin felt the tug of physical attraction.

But he had to go.

"They will accompany you to the border of Nicaragua," Maria Angela said. "From there you will be in the hands of the *Sandinistas*."

Gavin thought, If they ever found out who he worked for, things would get very interesting.

"You will eventually be smuggled into Florida," Maria Angela said. She suddenly seemed nervous. Her hands were white with pressure, her fingers twined together.

Time to go, Gavin thought.

Outside, the night air was humid and hot. Gavin wiped a mosquito from his forearm as he followed the two silent young men through the alley. He glanced back one time and saw the lights in the house blink off.

Duffy had been planning to telephone Marianne for weeks. She deserved better than him and he knew it. Still, she seemed to think that Duffy was a pretty special creature. He liked the feeling that gave him.

He had gotten unreasonably drunk at her last party, acted like a total asshole. The party itself was a semioffical Washington gathering. The new ambassador from a small African nation, the name of which Duffy couldn't remember, had been at the party, clothed in flowing robes, a small cylindrical cap on his head.

There had been two Scandinavians present as well, lovely blonde women whose cold blue eyes and long beautiful bodies had driven Duffy deeper into the bottle.

He had wound up taking a swing at a Polish diplomat and then falling down a flight of stairs. Marianne had been in tears before Duffy was finally bundled into a cab and sent home.

He should have called before now, he thought. He should have called the next day. But then everything seemed to fall apart. De Leon, his trip to Costa Bella, Gavin.

Gavin.

The thought of Gavin gave Duffy that same itch in his throat that was always soothed by whiskey. He hoped Gavin was still alive, but he wouldn't put his money on the possibility. Without Gavin, there wasn't a thing Duffy could do. There wasn't a helluva lot he could do even with Gavin.

Duffy tried to figure it out. The President had wanted a special report on Costa Bella. That was how it all started.

What did the President suspect? After all, the President already had the CIA report in front of him. There must have been something in that report that needed independent verification.

Duffy sighed. It was senseless to try to figure it out. All he knew was that one man was already dead because of it, and another man was in deep shit.

And what for? To discover that the regime in Costa Bella was corrupt? That it had existed on the backs of the people forever? That its military was bloodthirsty, never distinguishing between rebel forces and the population at large?

Those charges had been pretty well documented by the media; if the President watched television newscasts, he would have seen those themes beaten into the ground.

So why? Why a special report?

Duffy smiled. He knew why. Like every

other action taken in Washington, the basic motivation was: save your ass.

Someone wanted their ass saved, and if Duffy could find out who that person was, he'd have a much better idea of what it was all about.

thirteen _____

It had been forty-eight hours since Gavin had had any sleep.

He stood on the side of the road and gripped the small pack. The sun was just breaking over the horizon and it was already strong and warm.

He was standing at a bus stop on U.S. 1, which ran north-south along Florida's east coast. He was somewhere between Miami and West Palm Beach. That sixty-six-mile stretch of highway was nothing more than one long fast-food, gas station, and motel nightmare.

Gavin kept walking, and three blocks later he found a motel that had a vacancy. He checked in, paying in advance, and dead-bolted his room's door before crashing out on the soft, utterly comfortable bed.

When Gavin awoke, the room was chilled from the air conditioning. He sat up and pulled on his shirt. He fired a cigarette and shivered with the first full drag.

He checked his wristwatch. Five-thirty. He had slept through the day. He was hungry and dirty and when he rubbed a hand over his chin he felt the sharp stubble.

He walked to the window, the cigarette cupped in his hand. Tugging apart the drapes, he saw the gravel drive leading to the office.

There was a new black Continental outside the office. Gavin tried to squint through the glare off the office window. He could make out the clerk talking to two men, big beefy guys. One of the men was holding a sheet of paper.

Gavin let the drapes close except for a narrow opening. He didn't like the way the clerk seemed to be frightened.

The two men, wearing short-sleeved sport shirts, came out of the office and glanced at the door numbers around them. They finally settled on Gavin's door. He watched them as they moved towards the room, walking softly. He saw how their hands patted the thick bundles at their waistbands. As they closed in, one came towards the window and the other towards the door.

Gavin set the P-38 on single action. He let the drapes close completely. He quickly checked the bathroom. There was a small window set high up and no help whatsoever.

He heard the knock on the door.

Whoever they were, they didn't know

about that small, high bathroom window. There were only two of them, and they were both at the front of the building.

He gripped the P-38 in one hand and hoisted a heavy ashtray in the other. He threw it through the glass as hard as possible.

He heard a voice outside: "The back! Get around the back."

He heard the sounds of running feet and knew that the odds were now a lot better.

Gavin crossed the room and stood to one side of the door as one of the massive goons hurtled into the room, the door splintering ahead of him. He held a Magnum in his fist but his momentum carried him a few steps too far and when he recovered his balance and saw Gavin standing there it was too late. He tried to raise the Magnum but a 9mm round gave him a third eye before he could.

He sat down as if a puppet without strings and Gavin darted through the doorway and threw himself to the ground just as number two came skidding around the building, his .45 quivering in his hand.

Gavin placed a round in his heart with two shots. The first round took him high in the chest and he was still coming when the second round dropped him face first onto the gravel.

Gavin's heart was pounding. He ran

inside the motel room and checked the body for ID. There was none, nor any on the corpse in the courtyard.

Inside the office he saw the clerk had picked up the phone. Gavin ran to the office, reached out and plucked the receiver from the clerk's hand just as someone said, "Police department" on the other end of the line.

"In the car," Gavin said, motioning with the P-38. The clerk was a young, red-haired man with a bobbing Adam's apple, an underslung jaw, and slightly buckteeth. He was perhaps twenty-five years old.

"Aww shit," he said.

Gavin told him to drive and the kid backed the Continental around and exited on U.S. 1 heading north. Gavin kept the P-38 low and told the kid to keep driving.

Inside the car on the front seat was the sheet that they had been showing to the kid. Gavin picked it up and turned it over.

It wasn't a sheet of paper at all. It was a photograph of Gavin, and he recognized it immediately as his Agency photo. There wasn't much change; Gavin was easily identifiable from the photo.

How had those goons gotten this?

"Who were they?" He asked the red-haired driver.

"Couple of locals," he said. "Don't know what they wanted with you. They didn't say."

"Locals? You know them?"

"Sure. Billy and Jack Conlon."

"Billy and Jack Conlon. Who the hell are they?"

He shrugged. "They run pinball machines, video games, restaurant supplies. But they've always been hard dudes, you know. Real tough."

Gavin knew what he was hearing. Mob. Those two not only looked it, they sounded like it too. What the hell was the Mob doing after him? Equipped with an Agency photograph?

"Hold it here," Gavin said. If those two were local Mob, that meant that the authorities knew the car. They'd be suspicious if they saw the Conlon's Continental with two strangers in it.

The red-haired driver pulled over to the side of the road and stopped. There was no traffic on the side street they were on.

Gavin got out and told the driver to open the trunk. "Now get in," he said. He slammed the trunk shut and walked away from the Continental. Gavin's mind was racing. Bus and train stations were out, as well as airports. If they had guys checking motels, they'd definitely have those terminals locked up too.

When he got to U.S. 1 he stuck out his thumb and had a ride inside of ten minutes. It was a pickup truck driven by a farmer on his way back to Georgia. He drove Gavin straight through to Atlanta, and an hour later Gavin had scored a ride at a truck stop that took him within fifteen miles of Washington, D.C.

Gavin got a fistful of change and headed for the phone booth outside a roadside diner. The diner was set back from the road with a parking lot on its southern side. It was a log-cabin affair advertising EATS in neon above the Budweiser sign.

Gavin dialed the Justice Department and asked for Jack Duffy. It took four phone calls until he found a sympathetic switchboard operator who was willing to help him track down Duffy.

Then Duffy was on the line. "Hello?" he said.

"Good afternoon," Gavin said. "This is Johnston at American Express. Just calling to check that address again."

Duffy was quick. "Sure," he drawled into the phone. He gave Gavin his home address and then said, "I guess there won't be any more trouble with the account."

Gavin smiled. "You can count on it," he said, and hung up.

Gavin stepped from the phone booth and thought how nice it would be to lie down by the side of the road and sleep for about a day. He was exhausted, and he knew that he must look like a madman. His beard was overgrown and filthy-looking. His clothing was not much better. You can't live in the same clothing for days on end and not smell like it.

But that was all right. Soon he'd be able to shower and shave and get himself together. There was a lot of work to be done.

Someone had gone to a lot of trouble to turn Gavin's well-ordered life upside down. Someone had allowed Gavin to kill an innocent man, a friend. Someone didn't know Gavin very well or they wouldn't have done any of it. Gavin liked to keep things in balance, and they were way out of balance right now. He was going to even things up, and he didn't really care where the struggle took him.

He was his own man now, unemployed and damned near unloved. He had a few friends, and he was glad of it. He had some enemies too, and the thought did not make him unhappy. Someone had played him for a sucker, but they'd never do it again.

Barnes hated to use the same meeting place two times in a row. But he didn't want to argue. His position was not getting any stronger and he knew it. He walked through the doors of the Cafe Donato and saw his man in the back booth.

"This guy's a real terror," the coarse-faced man said as soon as Barnes sat down.

"You've got some news?" Barnes's heart

was pumping furiously. He had heard nothing about Gavin.

"Yeah, I got news," The man replied. "He's still alive. He's here. And he's armed."

The waiter came to the table and Barnes ordered a glass of white wine. "Tell me what happened," Barnes said as soon as the waiter left.

The other man shrugged. "All we know is that two guys near Fort Lauderdale tracked him to a motel but he took them both out and got away. We don't know were he is now. He could be anywhere."

Barnes' vision dimmed as the waiter placed the wineglass in front of him. His forehead was beaded with sweat and he swallowed hard before talking. "Are you sure it's the same man?"

"We're sure."

It seemed impossible. How had Gavin escaped from Costa Bella? And how had he entered the country?

"I suppose it's just a matter of time now," Barnes said.

"What do you mean?"

"I mean until your people pick up his scent again."

The other man grinned. "Hey, look. Don't depend on anything real fast. This guy is good; he knows what he's doing. He can stay out of sight for a long time. Sure, eventually we'll nail him. But not today. Not tomorrow."

Barnes swallowed half of his wine in one gulp. "I want my home watched night and day," Barnes said quickly. "He might come after me."

"We'll do what we can," the man said. He seemed bored by the discussion. Barnes was outraged.

"See here," Barnes said. "I need protection. I'm out here on a limb and I've got nowhere to go but to you people."

The other man grinned. "You paid your money and you took your chances. We'll do what we can."

Then he got up and left Barnes sitting there, his pulse rate much too fast, his head clammy with sweat.

Rojas was drunk.

He staggered to the metal door of the warehouse and opened it. Outside, the night was clear and cold and he stepped into the floodlit area outside the front door and waved at Ted, who was manning the gun tower that commanded a view of the road.

What good was money if he was a prisoner? Rojas hadn't been away from the warehouse since they arrived. What were the plans of the organization? Surely they recognized his value. All efforts should be made to return him to Costa Bella. He was useless here, Rojas thought.

He had no power, no men under his

control. He knew that he couldn't leave
the warehouse. Were he to be stopped by
any police unit, his lack of immigration
papers would insure his arrest.

Still, it was not all boredom and inactiv-
ity. He had begun a daily exercise hour
and he was feeling fit and ready for action.

There had been word from Washington
as well, and it looked as if he would be
leaving shortly.

But even more entertaining was the
delightful news he had received from Ted
only an hour earlier. Dr. Willard Lee was
coming to the warehouse, and they were
going to kill him.

Rojas wondered if the *americanos* would
mind if he did it himself. He needed a
little excitement in his life.

fourteen _____

Duffy lived in an apartment building near Watergate and when Gavin stepped out of the cab he realized just how seedy he looked.

He paid the cabbie, then argued with the security man at the door. The guy didn't even want to ring Mr. Duffy's apartment. Gavin pushed him back into the doorway and rang Duffy himself.

Duffy cleared it all up and moments later Gavin was stepping from the elevator on Duffy's floor. The hallway was done in red carpetlike material, giving it a suffocatingly close feeling. Gavin didn't like it.

Duffy's door was open and the moon-faced lawyer was smiling when he saw Gavin. "You look like shit," he said.

"Just get me a drink," Gavin said, slinging his pack onto an armchair, then sitting down on the sofa. He could feel the tension draining out of his shoulders and back. Duffy returned with a tall glass filled with Scotch and ice. He handed it to Gavin and watched as the ruggedly built intruder drained half the glass.

"How the hell did you get here?" Duffy asked. "The last word I had on you—and I had to figure it out for myself—was that ambush you were involved in."

"Yeah," Gavin said, wiping his mouth. The whiskey had warmed him and he let his legs sprawl out in front of him. "I didn't need that at all, but there it was. The rebels made it work. I was a dead man until they got involved."

"How did you get out of Costa Bella?"

"The rebels again. Sneaked me into Nicaragua, and from there to Cuba. I didn't have to do anything but sit in three different planes. It's wide open. Anyone can get into the country. I never realized how easy it is."

"OK. So now you're here. Now what? You know they released your name in the papers up here. No one had a photo of you—I guess the Agency didn't want to identify you as one of theirs, so they didn't release any photos either."

"Yeah?" Gavin fished his pack off the easy chair and dug out the photograph he'd taken from the Conlons' Continental in Florida. "Take a look at this. Surprising likeness, isn't it?"

Duffy swallowed. "What the hell is going on?" he asked.

"The guys I took this from were Mob.

They were after me, so I suppose there's a contract out—nationwide, judging that they were looking for me in Florida."

"And the picture?"

"Someone inside provided the picture. It makes sense. The whole deal has smelled bad from the start. I was a little too trusting. I didn't think the Agency would use me like they did. I didn't think they were that stupid."

"There are some good men in the agency."

"Yeah. I suppose so. Only I'm the guy wanted for murder, with the Mob conducting a nationwide hit search for me. I don't want to know about all the nice guys in the Agency."

Duffy was pacing the floor. "What the hell are you going to do now?"

Gavin grinned at him. "Make myself at home for a couple of days. Eat a few good meals, take a few showers, get some rest."

"Here?"

"Of course. Look, Duffy, you said you'd help. I don't have any other place to go. Not close by, anyway."

Duffy scowled. "You're right. I don't know what the hell I'm thinking about. You're safe here, of course. And I can do some legwork for you in the meantime."

"Good." Gavin dug in his pack again and came up with a scrap of paper. "Check out these aircraft markings. They belong to a new Cessna, a medical plane of some sort. Whoever owns that plane deserves a visit."

Duffy poured more Scotch into Gavin's glass. "First thing in the morning."

Gavin wiped his hand over his eyes. It was all catching up to him, the days without sleep, the unbearable tension of faceless assassins gunning for him. He'd made it to a safe haven, but now he could barely maintain consciousness.

He was asleep before he finished the second drink. Duffy lifted Gavin's legs onto the sofa, then hauled down a blanket from the bedroom closet and covered him.

Duffy knew it was going to be a hellish couple of days.

Barnes sat in his office at Langley and considered his options. Was it time to cut and run? He knew when he started out that it wouldn't go on forever. You can only play for a certain amount of time.

It had taken over two years to set up the drug connections. With Rojas and the other officials in Costa Bella, Barnes had a good deal going. Military men to convoy the drugs, an airborne medic to ferry them back to the States. His years with CIA had given him contacts in organized crime, dating back to the early sixties when the Agency involved the Mob in an attempt to assassinate Fidel Castro.

He brought in the drugs, they bought

the drugs from him. So far Barnes knew that he had over ten million dollars in Switzerland and he had enough phony ID to float the rest of his life.

But there was something he hadn't figured on. He didn't want to leave. He didn't want to give up the official power of life and death. He didn't want to leave the center of it all.

The money didn't mean that much anymore. At first it was all he lived for, the squirrellike accumulation of cash. But after the first few million, it lost all meaning to him.

He sighed. There was no doubt about it, however. He was going to have to cut and run. They'd never find him, of course. That was a pleasant thought. And he would be able to live a life that other men only dream of.

Brazil appealed to him. Slim, young dark boys in bikinis. Of course there were other places to visit, other bodies to sample.

He might even visit his friend Rojas in Costa Bella. He would be treated like a king there.

Barnes frowned. Rojas. Señor Rojas was a problem. There wasn't any easy way to get him back at the moment, though Barnes was sure something would work out. Not that he owed Rojas anything—the butcher had put away a small fortune himself, and

murdered uncounted people along the way
with glee.

Barnes stood up and glanced around the
office one last time. In a few minutes he
would leave, and no one would be aware of
any difference. His friends would wave
goodnight and the security guard would
smirk, noting Barnes' desires for him.

Then Barnes would be gone. They would
make a diligent search for him, but they
would find nothing. He knew how to cover
his tracks because he knew how the Agency
searched for people.

He knew all the tricks and he had a few
steps on them and that was all he needed.

Maria Angela rode in the back of the
troop transport along with four other
handcuffed, bloody civilians. They were
all afraid to talk to one another. They knew
why they were there, and they didn't want
to worsen their situation in any way.

Maria Angela almost smiled. When the
Security Police had arrived at her father's
home they had pushed the elderly man to the
floor. It no longer mattered that he was the
minister of the interior—his daughter was
wanted for questioning and that was that.

Maria Angela thought that it was perhaps the first time that her father had a
glimpse of the brutality that he helped
maintain in Costa Bella. Perhaps my death
will make a rebel out of him, she thought.

The Security Police had rounded up all known aquaintances of Colonel Rojas. There was talk of betrayal. Someone had led the rebels to Rojas, and the Security Police aimed to discover who had done it.

They would torture them all as a matter of course. Few would survive, and those that did probably would be better off dead.

When the truck stopped in the courtyard of the National Security Building, Maria Angela knew that there was only one thing to do. She broke from the ranks of prisoners and ran for the main gate. She heard the command to stop but that was not in her plans. When they opened fire from three different positions, Maria Angela was flung into the air and raked once again before she touched the ground.

Dr. Willard Lee had visited his attorney that afternoon. After brushing off remarks about how shaky he looked, Dr. Lee left a large manila envelope in his lawyer's hands, to be opened after his death. "I don't mean to be melodramatic," Dr. Lee had said to his lawyer.

"I'm used to it," Cramer grinned, hefting the envelope. He locked it in his safe while Dr. Lee watched.

Later, as Dr. Lee sprawled on the mat in front of the fireplace, his mind disintegrating under the effects of high-grade opium, he wondered how much longer he had left.

Money was no longer a problem. There was plenty of it.

He wouldn't even bother selling what was left of his private practice. It had fallen off in the last few years, and everyone had thought how wonderful he was to let a thriving practice run downhill while he flew missions of mercy for no pay.

One more thing to do and he was through. One last run up to Ojai and then Dr. Lee would pack his suitcases and take the first flight heading west.

He closed his eyes as he thought of what was awaiting him. Endless days and nights of near oblivion; he would be ministered to in every way by people who knew just what he wanted.

He stretched out and let the effects of the drug rush over him, thundering his consciousness, shattering it. He was breathing with an awful sound and somewhere in his mind the vestiges of the medical practitioner started making a diagnosis, but he shut off that awful voice and relaxed, sinking deeper into the drug, closing it all out.

Hours later he dressed and noticed that his hands weren't shaking any longer. He wore an open-neck shirt, wool pants, and heavy black shoes.

The Oldsmobile was better for the drive than the Buick, so he swung into the Cutlass and started the engine. It purred to

life and Dr. Lee smiled. He didn't want
any trouble, no problems to mar this last
bit of business.

He traveled slowly, in no rush. The traffic on the Ventura Freeway had eased up
after the rush hour, and he cruised at a
steady fifty-five, through the foothills near
Agoura, into the flat stretch leading to
the beach towns of Oxnard and Ventura.

He took the Ojai turnoff and marveled
at the clear skies. The mountains were
green and peaceful and Dr. Lee felt as if
he had finally done something right in
life.

He pulled up to the warehouse and waved
to Ted in the guard tower. He stepped into
the warehouse through the metal door and
saw Rojas sitting at the lone table, a bottle
of whiskey in front of him.

"Doctor," Rojas said clumsily, standing
up, supporting himself on the table. "So
good to see you. Please—sit down. Join me
in a drink."

"Delighted," Dr. Lee said. He sat down
across from Rojas and watched as the
smooth-skinned Latin poured out a hefty
amount of Irish whiskey.

"To your health," Rojas said, smiling.

Dr. Lee nodded and picked up his glass.
He tilted the hard edge against his lips
and just as the whiskey hit his gullet he
saw a flash of light and felt a thick uncomfortable intrusion somewhere in his torso.

He had been knocked backward out of the chair and as he rolled onto his side he saw Rojas stand up and look at him.

"My good doctor," Rojas said. "Is something wrong?"

Dr. Lee could see that the pistol in Rojas's hand was still smoking. He closed his eyes tight as a wave of pain made him soil himself. When he opened his eyes the room looked darker. Had someone turned off a light?

"Stop," Dr. Lee groaned. "You mustn't kill me. My lawyer—"

Rojas was standing next to him. The Latin knelt down so that he could hear what Dr. Lee was saying. "Your lawyer? What about your lawyer?"

"He knows everything," Dr. Lee gasped. "If I die he has instructions . . ."

"AAh. Just as in the famous gangster films," Rojas said, smiling. "Your insurance. What a shame." He put the .45 to Dr. Lee's head and said, "*Adios.*"

They buried Dr. Willard Lee in the soft ground near the water spigot that leaked.

fifteen _____

Duffy awoke early.

He checked Gavin, and saw that he was
still sleeping soundly. He fried two eggs,
prepared a pot of coffee on the automatic
coffee maker, then showered and dressed.
He was ready to leave thirty minutes later.
Gavin was stirring, so Duffy fried up two
more eggs and called Gavin to eat.

"I'll check out that airplane today," Duffy
said, watching as Gavin polished off the
eggs, then prepared two more. "If you want
me, call me at the office. I don't think
there's a wire on my line."

Gavin nodded. "Does any of this make
any sense to you?" He asked Duffy.

The moon-faced man sighed. "Not a
helluva lot," he said. "Hell, I just walked
into the middle of it."

"How so?"

"Direct Presidential order. He wasn't
satisfied with the official CIA report on
Costa Bella. He wanted to know if they'd
touched all the bases. The President com-

missioned me to launch an independent investigation of the situation there. That's how de Leon got pulled in. Then when de Leon was out of pocket, not reporting in, the President got nervous. Brought CIA back into it and told them to locate de Leon."

"Big mistake."

Duffy nodded. "Try telling that to the President. Anyway, the CIA no sooner got involved and de Leon gets arrested for the murders of the nuns and the priest."

"Set up for sure."

"But who's to know? Then you get sent down to kill him, which you do, and suddenly we're back to square one. Only you didn't do the rest of your deal. You were supposed to stand still and let them nab you and then maybe stand you up in front of a brick wall."

"Exciting thought, but I'm glad I missed it." Gavin wiped his mouth with a paper napkin decorated with little hearts.

"So it sounds like a lot of blood over nothing," Duffy said. "The President's back where he started; and I've got all kinds of people looking over my shoulder because I was called to the White House a few times and no one knows why."

"It'll all work out," Gavin said. "I've got nothing to do but make it work out, and I'm going to."

"Why not just head for the hills? You've

probably got an identity built up somewhere where they don't know Gavin from
mooseshit. Retire. Enjoy your life."

Gavin shook his head. "I can't let it go,"
he said. "Not only was de Leon a man I
knew—and admired—I've found out that
he was set up just like I was. Maybe his
death has no meaning—maybe no one's
death has a meaning—but I'm not going
to let this whole deal slide on a philosoph-
ical abstraction. I killed a man who didn't
deserve to die. Someone's going to pay for
that."

Duffy stood up and straightened his tie.
"Got to move out," he said. "I'll phone if I
catch anything spectacular."

Once Duffy was gone, Gavin ran a full
tub of hot water, let it cool a bit so as not
to scald himself, then slowly lowered himself into the steamy water. He felt the
grime and the grit rinse off his body and
cake the bottom of the tub. He closed his
eyes and felt drugged, the water smooth
and hot, the air cool and refreshing on his
face.

When the water cooled down he ran some
more, then washed thoroughly. When he
stepped from the tub he was as clean as a
man can get bathing by himself. He dried
off, then searched Duffy's closet for something to wear.

Duffy was pretty heavy but they were
about the same height. Gavin was delighted

to discover that Duffy's weight had come on recently. There was a full selection of shirts, pants, and jackets that Duffy would have to lose thirty pounds to wear, but which fit Gavin perfectly.

He dressed in a pair of dark blue wool trousers, a soft oxford striped shirt, and black plain-tip shoes. He walked back to the living room and flicked on the television. He watched the "Price is Right" and then a soap opera that had more violence in it than Gavin's life did.

Duffy tracked down the Cessna within an hour of arriving at the Justice Department. He was amazed at the file of Dr. Willard Lee. Humanitarian. Well-known southern California medical missionary.

There were other items in the file as well. Experience in Southeast Asia. Known involvement with drugs. An IRS investigation in the preliminary stages.

It could wait until Duffy went home, He didn't want to use the phone unless he had to, especially when he discovered that his efforts to track down the Cessna had provoked official interest.

Apparently the Cessna was flagged. Anyone asking for information on it was pegged. Duffy was waiting for the other shoe to drop. The IRS were real bastards.

When Duffy returned from a quick lunch

in the cafeteria he was told that the White
House had called.

Duffy returned the call and was told to
report immediately. He briefed his assistant, then took off for Pennsylvania Avenue.

He was shown into the Oval Office with
no more than a five-minute wait. Unheard
of.

Inside the President's office Duffy recognized Hafey from CIA. He'd never met
Arthur Hafey—the director rarely mixed
with beings of a lower order.

From behind his desk the President was
grinning at him, and Duffy knew that was
a bad sign. The President shared his grin
with Hafey, then asked Duffy to sit down.

"About time we let you in on something,"
The President said. "You've done a helluva
job for us. And we want to show our
appreciation."

"Well done," Hafey intoned.

"Are we talking about Costa Bella?" Duffy
asked.

"Sure are," the President drawled. "You
did just what we wanted. Flushed that bas-
tard out. Made him run."

"Good show," Hafey said.

Duffy checked out Arthur Hafey. Hafey
was an old-line intelligence man. He'd
signed on during the OSS days and had
trained in London during the war. He'd
picked up so many Briticisms that Duffy
sometimes thought Hafey had forgotten

he was an American. Clad in tweeds, smoking a pipe, his washed-out blue eyes blinking apologetically, Hafey looked like he would faint at the sight of blood. In fact, he was a thorough operator, with numerous night parachute jumps into Nazi territory to his credit.

Still, Duffy thought, if the Queen ever bent over in Hafey's presence, it was two to one that he'd kiss her ass.

"I hated to use you like that," the President said. Then he shrugged. "Sometimes I've got to," he continued. "And this time I feel good about it. It worked."

"What worked?" Duffy asked.

"Allow me, Mr. President," Hafey said. He turned his blue eyes on Duffy and said, "When we did our work in Costa Bella we discovered something going on. We couldn't really get into it without tipping our hand." He paused. "You see, it concerned our man in charge of Costa Bellan intelligence. It was his show. We couldn't make a move without tipping him off."

Duffy was beginning to catch on.

"So we talked the President into launching a separate investigation. At the right moment we would let our man know that the operation was going on. Then we would watch him."

Duffy was thinking fast. "So the entire de Leon thing was a smoke screen?"

Hafey nodded. "Indeed. We had to have

something that looked real. After all, it would have to fool a very able and intelligent Agency man."

The President picked it up. "So when you told me that de Leon was missing, I contacted Hafey and we decided it was as good a pretense as we needed to bring Barnes into it."

"Barnes?" Duffy was trying to think straight.

"Barnes was our man in Costa Bella for years," Hafey said. "When he returned to Washington we put him in charge of the Central American desk. He ran all the operations personally. We had to spook him. Make him nervous. If he was guilty, we wanted him to feel pressure. Make a mistake."

"And he did," the President said. "We knew as soon as the news reached us about de Leon that he had been framed. Nothing works out that coincidentally."

"Then why didn't we step in and stop it? Why did De Leon have to die?"

Hafey answered him. "Because we needed time to let it work in Barnes. That's why he was given the task of eliminating de Leon. We wanted as much pressure on him as we could bring to bear. And it worked."

"It worked?" Duffy's mind was racing. What had worked? De Leon was dead, Gavin was a marked man, and all for what?

Hafey exchanged a satisfied glance with the President. "Barnes broke and ran," he said. "Didn't show up at Langley this morning. We checked out his apartment. He's gone, all right. Probably has something to do with that man Gavin. I think Gavin spooked him more than we did."

"And what about Gavin?" Duffy demanded to know.

"Not much we can do for him," Hafey said. "You know how it is. We can't stand up for him. He's on his own out there, just like other men in his situation. It goes with the job."

"Besides," The President said, "We really don't have much use for men like Gavin when we're through with them. After all, what is he? A paid killer, more or less. Now of course I realize that he killed in his country's name, but when you farm out a man like that, sometimes you've got a time bomb on your hands, liable to go off at any moment."

"He'll never get out of Costa Bella alive anyway," Hafey said, yawning. "Tightest security in Central America. He's a dead man already."

Duffy was smiling.

sixteen _____

Gavin was kicked back on the sofa when Duffy walked in. The nightly news was on and Gavin had a Scotch and water in his hand.

"You look like somebody slapped you around," Gavin said. "Tough day at the office?"

Duffy fixed a drink for himself. He had to tell Gavin what had happened, there was no two ways about that. He sat opposite Gavin, in the easy chair, and began to talk.

Fifteen minutes later he sat back. He'd broken out in a sweat as he watched the expression harden on Gavin's face. Any thoughts Duffy had of talking Gavin out of his search-and-destroy mission faded when he looked at that face.

"So that's it," he said finally. "Barnes." He tossed down the rest of his drink and stood up. "Burned everyone and got away clean."

"Don't look at it that way," Duffy said,

giving it one last shot. "They'll call off that heat on you—I finally got them to go that far. Only they don't want to hear from you ever again. Or hear about you ever again. Just go off somewhere and get yourself a new life."

"Sure," Gavin said. "Only I have to sleep nights and I don't want to have to drink a quart of Scotch in order to do it. This is my business and I'll settle it."

"Let it lie," Duffy said. He was getting angry. What the hell was he doing in the middle of this? He had a nice secure little thing going, and he didn't want to be blown out of the water.

"Look," Gavin said. "I know how you feel. I appreciate all the help you've given me all the way down the line. Someday if you ever need help you'll know where to turn. And you'll know that I'll go right to the end of it with you."

Duffy thought, Aw shit. There was no talking to the man. He had his own code and he wasn't going to stop. Duffy sighed and fished around in his coat pocket. "OK then," he said. "Here's the information on the Cessna. The file was flagged because there's an upcoming IRS operation about to come down on the good doctor."

Gavin took the material eagerly. He read it quickly, then sat back. "Clever," he said. "Very clever."

"Hafey said that the operation was ongoing for a couple of years. That's a lot of drugs."

Gavin nodded. "Sure. Transhipped in from Peru and Colombia, then moved slowly into this country via the good doctor. Maybe netting a half million or so a flight. Over the years that makes Barnes, Lee, and Rojas very rich men."

"Barnes knew it was coming down. Hafey says that Barnes probably had perfect escape routes laid out. He knew the Agency so well there's not a damned chance of them finding him."

"That's just because they don't want to look," Gavin said quietly.

Duffy squirmed. "They did mention something about letting sleeping dogs lie . . ."

"Sure. They'd rather kiss off the deal and not have to confront it. They got him out and they got him running, and he's no longer a danger to them. They don't care what happens to him and they know they can be embarrassed if word of this gets out."

"They don't want the story to get out."

"Of course not. A top CIA official implicated in a drug deal with officials of the Costa Bellan Government? What chance would the military have if that story got out? There's plenty of opposition right now about American involvement in Central America. Congress would never go for it if this story were made public."

Duffy almost didn't want to ask the question. "Will you go public with it?"

Gavin laughed. "I don't care what they do," he said coldly. "Influencing international events is something I leave to guys who wear glasses and carry signs that say No More Nukes. I have no interest at all in anything except watching Barnes squirm in the dirt at my feet and beg for mercy."

Duffy nodded. "I guess you'll be going," he said.

Gavin stood up. "There's still plenty of Mob heat after me. That contract's still in effect. I'd appreciate you pulling some strings for me."

"Name it."

"Get me on a military flight to a West Coast base. If I know Barnes, he's out there, cleaning up that end of his operation, positive that he's got plenty of time to work with. He knows damned well the agency won't come after him because there's always the possibility that the newspapers will get a hold of it."

"I'll do what I can," Duffy said.

Gavin was already stuffing papers into his pack. "I'll be ready whenever you are," he said.

The airmen were a friendly bunch aboard the C-147. They were loaded out of their skulls—Gavin had seen them passing a joint around just before takeoff.

It didn't bother him. He'd known too many fighter pilots who never felt they were flying well unless they had some booze in them. If it all came down to a sudden fiery end because someone smoked a joint—well, life and death sometimes hinges on a lot less.

It was an uneventful flight. The airmen left Gavin alone and he used the time to sort out his thinking. He'd been tempted to take the government's offer and retire. Get back to High Card, Colorado, and start a life for himself. In High Card he was Bob Evans, and no one except Nick Coletti knew that he was there.

And there was Kendall. She deserved better than the kind of life he was going to have to lead. He loved her, but he had to follow his own instincts.

And in this case his instincts told him that he'd never have any peace if he didn't finish this deal.

He was sleeping when the airman nudged him awake and told him that they were fifteen minutes out of Edwards Air Force Base in the High Desert. Gavin yawned and belted himself in.

He watched as the ground lights came up to meet him and then jolted a bit when the big bird set down. It was still East Coast time on his wristwatch and he set it back three hours as he exited the transport.

Gavin got a ride into Los Angeles with

two airmen on leave. He traded war stories with them and told them that he was
a magazine writer on special assignment.

He checked into an oceanfront hotel
called the Sea Breeze in Santa Monica a
block south of the intersection of Wilshire
and Pico. Once in his room he dug out his
paperwork and noted Dr. Willard Lee's
address.

It was as good a place to start as any.
He felt a bit more comfortable. Mob activity on the West Coast was not as intense
as it was on the East Coast. And southern
California was a large area to cover.

Gavin rented a Ford LTD and felt like a
successful businessman as he cruised to
the doctor's house. It was a bright sunny
day, cooler than it appeared, and Gavin
realized that for the first time in a long
time he felt good.

The doctor's house appeared deserted.
Gavin parked in the long, winding driveway
and rang the door chimes. They echoed
inside and he knew the place was empty.
He walked around the house and saw that
the kitchen door was a flimsy affair, easily opened. He checked for security wires,
found them, and worked around them. Ten
minutes later he was inside, the smell of
decay strong in the stale air.

Dr. Lee had been gone for a while. He
checked out the doctor's desk and found
an address book. There was a notation on

the desk calender that interested Gavin:
Info. to Cramer, it said. It was dated two
days earlier.

He checked through the address book
until he found a notation for Cramer.
Attorney at law, it said. Cramer was Lee's
lawyer, and Lee saw him a few days ago.

He also gave him—or left with him—
information. Gavin knew what he would
do in Lee's situation, with his life coming
down around his ears: make some life
insurance for himself. And giving your
lawyer incriminating information was the
oldest way to do it.

One of the most ineffective too, Gavin
thought. Lee wasn't dealing with normal
people. They didn't care what anyone knew
or didn't know.

The first time that lawyer tried to make
that information public he'd have agents
from the FBI, the CIA, and the DSA in his
office. In no uncertain terms they would
tell him not to reveal a word of any of it
under pain of a national security violation.

They would confiscate the papers and
that would be that.

Gavin locked up and got back into the
LTD and headed for Cramer's office. It was
still a pleasant day, and he flicked on the
radio and listened to Dr. Toni Grant dis-
pense psychological advice over a wide
range of subjects. He liked her voice and

wondered what she sounded like talking face to face.

When he arrived at Cramer's office he saw two thickset men in sports clothes loitering near the elevator. He took the stairs to the third floor and walked down the hall till he came to Cramer's office. He let himself in and smiled at the pretty black receptionist. "Is Mr. Cramer in?" Gavin asked pleasantly.

"Do you have an appointment?" she asked sweetly.

Gavin hauled out the Walther P-38 and motioned her to Cramer's door with it. She opened the door and they both entered the private office.

"See here—" Cramer was upset at the sight of the pistol.

"I'll keep it simple," Gavin said. "Dr. Willard Lee came in here a few days ago and perhaps left some papers with you. Let's have them, if you please."

Cramer bridled. He wasn't used to being ordered around. "Not a chance," he said. "The relationship between an attorney and his client is confidential. Protected by law."

Gavin knew that there was only one way to go. He raised the automatic, sighted carefully, and blew off Cramer's left earlobe.

The receptionist passed out cold, crumbling to the floor. Cramer sat as if hit across the forehead with a baseball bat.

Blood gushed down his shirt front and he looked like he was going to cry.

"The whole deal is, give me the papers," Gavin said. The wound was minor and Cramer would be laughing about it in a few days.

Maybe.

Gavin sighted once again and this time Cramer was on his feet, holding up his hand. "OK, OK," he said. "Just put down the gun, mister."

Gavin watched as Cramer twirled the dial on the wall safe, opened it up, then withdrew a large manila envelope. IIe handed it to Gavin.

"That's all of it," he said.

"Sit down." Gavin said.

Cramer collapsed in his chair. "Now as soon as I walk out of here you're going to get on the phone and call the cops. I don't blame you. Right now you're real hot and you want to get even.

"Now, even if the police get here in record time—and we both know what the odds are on that—the chances are that I'll be gone.

"But if they do get here real fast and I see them I'll dump the pistol and walk right by them and come back here some day and fiddle around with you some more."

"What do you want me to do?" Cramer asked in a dispirited voice.

"Take your time making that call. Let's keep it as painless as possible for both of us." Then he turned and walked out of the office.

He was downstairs and out of the building twenty seconds later. There was no sign of the two toughs who'd been hanging around the elevators.

Gavin drove back to the beach, turned to car in at the hotel rental booth, and went to his room. He spread out the papers on the bed and saw there was plenty of reading to do.

He prepared a whiskey and water, lighted a Marlboro, and sat on the edge of the bed as he began reading the writings of Dr. Willard Lee.

It was all there. The entire operation, from conception to execution. It had all been Barnes', all the way. He set it up while he was assigned to Costa Bella in the sixties. Rojas ran it down there, and between them they'd split millions of dollars.

They were warehousing the drugs near Ojai. Gavin dug out his road map and checked it out. It appeared to be about a two-hour drive from Los Angeles.

Would they be waiting for him? Probably. Barnes was aware that Gavin had returned, and he knew Gavin well enough to know that anything was possible once Gavin got the scent.

There was a knock on the door and Gavin

eased the P-38 from his jacket pocket and stood off to the side of the door.

"Who's there?" Gavin asked.

It was a shotgun blast that would have cut him in half had he been standing in front of the door. He pumped two rounds back through the splinters and saw one man's head explode into red meat.

The other guy turned tail and ran and Gavin stepped out into the hall and pumped three rounds into his back and watched as he skidded to a stop on his face, his left foot ticking away the last beats of his heart.

Gavin walked back inside the room and picked up the papers and stuffed them into his pack. Behind the door to the room was a sign that said CHECK OUT: NOON.

Did he have a refund coming?

seventeen _____

Gavin was three blocks from the hotel when he heard the first sirens. The hotel would be able to give a fairly accurate description of him, but that description would fit so many men that it would be worthless.

Tonight hundreds of thousands of southern Californians would watch the evening news coverage of the killings. Beach Massacre—More at Eleven. People would shake their heads and blame their own particular scapegoat for the continued breakdown in Law and Order.

Fifteen minutes after leaving the hotel, Gavin spotted a beat-up '71 TR-6. He was familiar with the ignition set-up on the early seventies' models of the popular British sports car. Reaching underneath the steering column Gavin gripped the ignition housing and twisted it off. The connection could be made by inserting and twisting a screwdriver. Gavin made it work with a ballpoint pen instead. He drove directly to the Santa Monica Freeway and made it to the juncture of the San Diego Freeway a few minutes later. Gavin took the Bakersfield ramp, circled up above the San Diego on the connecting ramp, then dropped down and merged with the heavy northbound traffic. The freeway followed the route of the earlier—and still functioning—Sepulveda Boulevard, cutting through the mountains into the San Fernando Valley yawning in front of him as he topped the climbing freeway at Mullholland Drive.

There was a thick layer of brown air hanging over the valley, which, Gavin noticed as he dove down into it, smelled like a soup made of motor oil, old carburetors, and chopped tires. There was no air conditioning in the cramped TR-6. There was nothing for Gavin to do except keep the windows down and enjoy.

He took the exit for the Ventura Freeway, swung around the curve, and joined the lighter traffic moving in a northwesterly direction. Gavin rode the Ventura Freeway to the small beach town of Ventura, then exited at a roadside Denny's.

Gavin took his pack with him into the brightly lit color-coordinated restaurant. He took a seat in a booth by the door and ordered a cheeseburger, fries, and coffee. Then he opened his map on the table.

Ojai was almost due north of where he sat. He saw that the access roads to the

town were small state roads. Ojai sat on
the edge of the Los Padres National Forest—
easy enough to get lost in.

Gavin ate quickly and had two cups of
coffee. He was anxious to get back to it.
He wanted to finish it as quickly as possible.

Forty-five minutes later he was in Ojai,
a sun-dappled community with the charm
of a turn-of-the-century dream of an American village. There were service stations
enough to mar the effect, and Gavin left
the TR-6 parked at one that was closed.

Dr. Lee's documents gave the exact loca-
tion of the warehouse where the drugs
were stored before transshipment to the
American buyers, a family in the East
Coast mob structure that operated in New
York City.

Gavin set out on foot. He walked due
north, finally cutting away from the road
and hiking into the hills. It took him perhaps twenty minutes to reach the small
crest marked by a radio tower. From there,
according to Dr. Lee, the warehouse would
be visible.

It was.

Gavin was flattened out, peering around
the crestline scrub. Below, in the next valley, sat the warehouse. It was serviced by
a two-lane dirt road. At one time the warehouse had been part of a milling operation.

The gun tower, however, was a new addi-
tion to the warehouse's rustic charm. That,

and the steel door that glistened in the side of the warehouse facing Gavin.

There was a closed garage attached to the warehouse. It probably had an automatic door as well.

Gavin could see a kennel enclosure off to the side of the warehouse. The Dobermans inside were probably used for night security. For now they were safely out of the way.

Gavin saw a figure on the hill opposite him. He pulled his binoculars out and checked. The man was carrying a Thompson submachine gun. He wasn't looking for quail.

One in the tower, one on the hill opposite. That meant there should be a third working Gavin's side of the valley. He checked left and right and saw nothing.

Then he heard him coming up behind.

The sentry had apparently crossed the crestline and was working his way back. Long hours of fruitless surveillance had made him noisy through carelessness.

Gavin eased around and saw that the sentry would probably pass thirty yards or so from Gavin's position. It was too early to tangle with them, he decided. He wanted to check out the situation a bit more carefully. The three sentries might not be all the firepower present.

When the sentry got to the top of the hill he was only twenty yards from Gavin, but he wasn't even looking in Gavin's direction. He carried a Mark II sten gun, but didn't look comfortable handling it. Gavin wondered why they didn't carry shotguns. Much less obvious—they could always say they were after rabbits. It's hard to explain away a sten gun if by chance a state trooper drives by and happens to see it.

As soon as the sentry started his descent, Gavin crawled back to the rim of the hill and studied the valley. He knew he had to move before they turned to dogs loose. The Dobermans in the dark, would be awesome.

The steel door to the warehouse opened and Rojas stepped out in the waning afternoon sunlight. He was dressed in his Costa Bellan battle fatigues. He wore a .45 on his belt. He stood with his fists on his hips, legs widespread. He glanced at the man in the gun tower, then directed his gaze toward the sentry coming down the hill from Gavin's direction.

Gavin lay perfectly still. He was as low as possible, peering through scrub brush. As he watched, he saw the doorway fill with another figure, smaller than Rojas. When the figure moved out into the sunlight, Gavin grinned.

Barnes.

He looked uncomfortable in the open spaces. Offices suited the small man nicely. Here, he walked tentatively, as if the

ground were going to open up and swal-
low him. He shaded his eyes with his hand,
peering in different directions. Some guys
can't function in an environment that isn't
artificially controlled. Take away the air
conditioning, the elevators, and the smoothly functioning computers and video screens
and you take away their reality. Gavin
could see the threatened expression on
Barnes' face. It was like nature was holding a gun on him.

Gavin watched as the two sentries who'd
been working the hills made their way
down to Rojas. The blond guy in the gun
tower came down, and then they turned
loose the Dobermans.

Gavin moved quickly, down the hill away
from the warehouse. He ran as soon as
the terrain was safe enough. Twenty minutes later he was in the village.

They let the dogs loose earlier than he
had figured. He was going to have to make
his move early in the day when the ani-
mals were locked up.

The TR-6 sat in the service station. It
had attracted no attention. He slid into
the driver's seat, started up the sports car
and headed down the road toward Ventura. He would spend the night there and
try again in the morning.

Rojas was ready to explode from boredom. "Just one night," he pleaded with

Barnes. "What harm can there be in it? I must get out of here, sit down somewhere, have a few drinks, a good meal, perhaps a woman . . ."

"A woman is out of the question."

"Then just the drinks and a meal. Ted will accompany me. We will be perfectly all right."

Barnes didn't like it. He didn't like it because things can go wrong very easily. Still, Rojas was a madman, and he seemed to be quite serious about it. If Barnes said no, then Rojas would more than likely challenge him. Barnes didn't want that.

"Very well, Rojas. I will remain here, as you say. I have no need to go." Barnes chuckled. "And I hope indeed that you have a very enjoyable evening." Then his face became stern. "But no women. Women are trouble. You can wait till you return to Costa Bella for that!"

Ted drove the Cadillac. He told Rojas that there was a good steak joint in Ventura, where they would relax over a few stiff drinks before digging into two-pound steaks with all the trimmings. "And the waitresses? Are they beautiful?" Rojas asked.

"All they got is waiters," Ted answered.

Gavin checked in at the Pierpont Inn, easily the classiest hotel in Ventura. There is always less heat in the best places, and for someone driving a stolen car and wanted for murder, no place was too good.

Room service provided a full menu, but Gavin decided to go out to eat. What he needed, he thought, was a good old-fashioned chowdown. That, plus a good night's sleep. Nothing like it to tune up a man's system, have him ready to eat fire in the morning.

He left the Triumph parked in the Pierpont Inn lot and walked down the curving drive that led to the beachfront. There he headed north, walking along the beach. Ahead was a Holiday Inn, built right on the beach. But to his right was a restaurant that looked like a Colorado road house—small, low-slung, dark wood exterior and a parking lot filled with pick-ups and four-wheel drive vehicles.

The restaurant—Gavin saw that the name of the place was Chuck's—was across the street from Gavin. He sat down on a concrete bench and lit a Marlboro. He'd wait until the place emptied a bit. He wanted to take his time with his meal and that was almost impossible in a crowded steak joint.

He noticed the Caddie as soon as he lighted his cigarette. Black, new, with opaque windows. He watched as it turned into Chuck's parking lot and zipped into a space toward the rear of the building, deep in shadow.

Rojas got out.

Gavin hunched lower on the bench, tucking his chin down. He flicked the Marlboro onto the ground. Another man, blond and husky, got out from the driver's side. Both men entered the restaurant.

The monster gets a meal.

Gavin's heart was racing. He crossed the street and walked up the driveway into the parking lot. There were no attendants. He tightened his grip on his pack. When he got to the Caddie he inspected the trunk, the directed a sharp kick about two inches above the trunk lock.

The trunk opened.

Gavin considered the situation.

If he attacked during the day he had to dispose of at least three armed sentries before he could get his hands on Rojas and Barnes.

At night, he was faced with the Dobermans.

Or he could allow himself to be driven into the area and take his chances once inside.

He figured quickly. There was a small grocery store next to the restaurant and he walked through it quickly, selecting cold cuts, bread, and a bottle of Scotch. He walked back to the parking lot, climbed inside the trunk of the Caddie, and closed the trunk door after him.

It was going to be a long night.

eighteen _____

Riding in the trunk of a car, even if it is a Cadillac, is not the answer. Gavin shifted uncomfortably as the Caddie bounced off the paved road and began to trek toward the warehouse on the graded dirt road.

Gavin had worked his way through half the bottle of Scotch and was feeling fine, except for the unexpected bumps of the road. He held the P-38 in his one fist and whenever the Caddie slowed enough, he tilted the bottle of J&B to his lips.

He was warm and loose and he didn't much give a damn if they opened the trunk or not. Whoever opened the trunk would die first, of course. Gavin would waste him and hope that the surprise of his attack would carry the day. But what he wanted was for the blond driver to park the Caddie, and for Rojas and the blond to go inside and leave Gavin all alone.

As the Caddie bounced down the road, Gavin thought about Kendall, snug in High Card. He felt a sudden cold, wanton emptiness. What the hell was he doing? He had a life in High Card, a comfortable, warm and secure hidaway, and a beautiful blue-eyed woman named Kendall who thought she'd never met a man as desirable as he was.

Gavin took another hit from the bottle of J&B and wondered if he'd ever see her again.

He heard the gravel crunching under the tires and realized they'd entered the warehouse area. The Caddie rolled to a stop and paused for perhaps ten seconds, then rolled forward again.

It was the blond driver opening the automatic door to the garage.

Gavin heard the two men exit the Caddie and slam their doors. He heared their footsteps, cold and clangy against the concrete garage floor.

Then there was silence.

Gavin gave it thirty minutes, then he worked the lock and popped open the trunk. He came out quietly, then closed the trunk.

The garage was dark and cold. He stood up, stretching, getting the blood flowing. He was stiff and awkward and he needed to get loose.

Gavin knew he was a bit blasted from the Scotch but he figured that it all evened out. What he gave up in the way of instant reflexes he gained from relaxation. He felt good and he wanted to work out.

There was a door that led to the warehouse proper. It was a composition cheapie, and Gavin could hear them in the next room.

They were talking about poor Dr. Willard Lee. Gavin smiled when he heard Rojas describe how he'd suckered the doctor with a drink.

Rojas was going to be fun.

Gavin felt warm, his muscles loose and tingling. He hefted the P-38 and walked towards the door.

He paused, breathing easily. There were probably five of them in the next room. Rojas, Barnes, the blond, and two others, the guys who'd been walking the hills. Maybe there were more.

It didn't matter. There wasn't much to think about, except that when he went through the door he hoped he was the only one holding a gun.

Gavin twisted the door handle and pulled.

The light flooded his eyes as he bolted into the room. Things were in that half-real state of semi-slow motion, brought on by immersion in a charged, dangerous situation. Gavin's senses were on alert and he had the step on the five men in the warehouse.

"Freeze!" Gavin yelled. He wanted them to lock up. Once he had them under the gun they'd be easier to deal with. After all, no one wants to be the first man to die. And once he had them, whoever went for it first would definitely eat it. But in order to make that work he had to freeze them.

He failed.

One of the sentries—the one who'd been walking Gavin's hill earlier—rolled off the bunk and came up with the sten gun. He came up a bit too fast, however, exposing his head first.

Gavin's first shot took him through the nose and he thrashed on the floor for a while before dying.

But Gavin was moving too quickly to see that. The others were all moving, taking advantage of the sentry's self-sacrifice, making their plays.

The blond man who'd driven the Cadillac was easy. He stood in the middle of the room and tried to click off the safety on a shotgun with fingers that suddenly seemed thick and clumsy because Gavin's second shot entered his forehead above his right eye. He fell suddenly, lifeless before he banged onto the floor.

Meanwhile there was another sentry and Rojas. Barnes had moved quickly to the steel door leading outside and when Gavin directed a round in his direction it bounced harmlesssly off the closing metal door.

Gavin took out the overhead light with

his fourth shot and the warehouse plunged into darkness.

In the darkness Gavin could hear the dogs barking outside as they caught Barnes' scent. He imagined the horror the desk-bound Barnes must be feeling in the darkness with the sharp-toothed Dobermans.

Inside, a shot rang out, sparking the wall to the left of Gavin. He peered through the darkness, his eyes adjusting to the shadows. He saw a shape loom in front of him and he fired twice, rolling to his right as soon as he did. Gavin heard a gurgling noise and then the sound of a body crumpling to the floor. There was a wet moan and a harsh cry for help.

That left Rojas.

Gavin heard a low gentle laugh from the other side of the warehouse. "My congratulations," Rojas soothed. "You are an exceptional man, my friend. A man I would have been proud to number among my friends."

Gavin crawled forward. He peered through the darkness but the distances in the warehouse were too great. He could see nothing.

"Perhaps you should reload," Rojas continued. "I wish you to have every chance." The low laughter purred out to Gavin.

"Here is something for you," Rojas said. He opened up with an automatic rifle, sending a burst across the warehouse. Gavin lay absolutely still. Automatic fire didn't turn him on at all.

Gavin knew that Rojas was in the far corner. He listened carefully. He heard soft movements, and he silently edged to his left, circling the advancing Rojas.

At the last moment he ducked low under a window and watched as Rojas, across the room, failed to do so. For a moment the Costa Bellan beast was illuminated in the moonlight and as Gavin squeezed off a shot he heard Rojas grunt with the impact. Then Gavin hit the deck again as Rojas fired a last burst, knocking out the window above Gavin's head and showering him with thousands of glass splinters.

Rojas slumped to the floor. Gavin could hear his wet, noisy breathing. He eased farther to his left, coming in behind Rojas.

Ahead of him Gavin could see that Rojas was on the floor, his AK-47 still gripped in his hand. He was conscious, but barely so. He was waiting for Gavin to make a move.

Gavin came up behind him and kicked away the rifle then leaned in close. "Rojas," he said. "Are you afraid to die?"

Rojas turned his head and looked Gavin in the eyes and laughed in his face. Gavin lodged the Walther in Rojas' ear and pulled the trigger.

Outside, the dogs were enjoying their dinner.

* * *

Two hours later Gavin took a pocketful
of dimes into a public phone booth near
the Santa Monica Pier and called newspapers, including the *Los Angeles Times*.
He told the night editor that he would
find a few million dollars worth of hard
drugs and various bodies in a warehouse
just outside of Ojai. He told the night editor that one of the bodies was that of a
Costa Bellan Army officer.

Then Gavin hung up and began hitch-
hiking toward Colorado.

It took two days for the story to break
open. The local authorities tried to sit on
it, but the newsmen had been there first
and they decided to publish against the
wishes of the government.

They agreed to keep Barnes' identity
quiet. There wasn't much left of him to
identify. The Dobermans had been hungry.

Duffy read the account on page two of
the *Washington Post*. Five dead men, more
drugs that most narcs had ever seen in
one place, and the evident involvement of
the Costa Bellan authorities in the entire
mess.

Page one of the *Washington Post* detailed
the President's decision to hold off supplying more arms to the government of
Costa Bella. The United States had come
down on the side of a negotiated settle-

ment and the United States didn't seem to mind that the decision meant curtains for the current regime.

Duffy wondered if he would ever hear from Gavin again.

In the spring of 1878 Charlie O'Neill and Jesse Kendall decided to call off their partnership. It was a case of cabin fever, pure and simple. The two gruff prospecters had spent the winter holed up in a cabin and they'd gotten their fill of each other. They decided that as soon as the weather permitted, one of them would leave, signing over his half of the silver claim to the other.

They decided who was to stay by drawing cards. High card got to stay. Kendall drew the jack of diamonds and laughed when O'Neill came up with the eight of spades. Jesse Kendall then owned the mine outright, and he watched a small town develop around his claim. High Card, Colorado, hadn't changed a whole lot since then. That was why Gavin liked it.

Bob Evans was the name they knew him by in High Card and he didn't see any reason to change it. It had taken a week to work his way back to High Card. His beard was already coming in when he arrived.

He went directly to Dorn's garage, had a few drinks with the hulking mechanic, then watched as Dorn opened his safe and handed over the envelope stuffed with hundred dollar bills. three hundred and seventy of them; all the money Gavin had.

Gavin phoned Kendall from Dorn's. She got so excited she dropped the phone and ran down Main Street and came bursting into Dorn's scruffy office as Gavin sat there, still holding the receiver in his hand.

He stayed with Kendall in the small apartment over the book store for a week before returning to his cabin on the foothill. He figured he'd give the place a paint job, then kick back and let some time pass.

Life was good. He hadn't had a gun in his hand since the night in Ojai, and he didn't miss it a bit. Sometimes when he and Dorn sat on the deck looking at the mountain and the sun sliding down behind it Gavin would bring out a bottle of Scotch and let Dorn tell him about his travels, his adventures, and his women.

From the deck he could see the light in Kendall's window.